MEN AND GODS

This outstanding collection brings together the novelist and scholar Rex Warner's knack for spellbinding story-telling with Edward Gorey's inimitable talent as an illustrator in a memorable modern recounting of the most beloved myths of ancient Greece.

Writing in a relaxed and winning colloquial style, Warner vividly recreates the classic stories of Jason and the Argonauts and Theseus and the Minotaur, among many others, while Gorey's quirky pen-and-ink sketches offer a visual interpretation of these great myths in the understated but brilliantly suggestive style that has gained him admirers throughout the world. These tales cover the range of Greek myth-ology, including the creation story of Deucalion and Pyrrha, the heroic adventures of Perseus, the fall of Icarus, Cupid and Psyche's tale of love, and the tragic history of Oedipus and Thebes. *Men and Gods* is an essential and delightful book with which to discover some of the key stories of world literature.

ALSO PUBLISHED BY
NEW YORK REVIEW BOOKS

The Haunted Looking Glass
Edited and illustrated by Edward Gorey

The War of the Worlds
By H.G. Wells
Illustrated by Edward Gorey

Men and Gods

Myths and Legends of
the Ancient Greeks

REX WARNER

Illustrated by Edward Gorey

New York Review Books
New York

THIS IS A NEW YORK REVIEW BOOK
PUBLISHED BY THE NEW YORK REVIEW OF BOOKS
1755 Broadway, New York, NY 10019
www.nyrb.com

Library of Congress Cataloging-in-Publication Data
Warner, Rex, 1905–1986.
  Men and gods : myths and legends of the ancient Greeks / by Rex
Warner ; illustrations by Edward Gorey.
    p. cm. — (New York review books classics)
  Originally published: New York : Farrar, Straus and Young, 1951.
  ISBN-13: 978-1-59017-263-6 (alk. paper)
  ISBN-10: 1-59017-263-9 (alk. paper)
  1. Mythology, Greek. I. Title.
BL783.W37 2007
398.20938—dc22

                              2007031162

ISBN 978-1-59017-263-6

Printed in the United States of America on acid-free paper.
10 9 8 7 6 5 4 3 2 1

To Jonathan Warner

CONTENTS

CONTENTS

Men and Gods

Pyramus and Thisbe

PYRAMUS and Thisbe lived next door to each other in the city of Babylon, which Semiramis is said to have walled all round with brick. Pyramus was a most beautiful young man and Thisbe more lovely than all the girls of the East. As they were neighbors they soon got to know each other, and in the end they fell in love. They ought really to have got married, but their parents forbade them to do so. What they could not forbid was that they should be in love, which they were, one as much as the other. They had no one to help them in their secret and could only talk together by nods and gestures; but the more their feelings were hid, the more desperate their hidden feelings became.

In the wall between their two houses there was a small chink which had been left there by the builders. Nobody had noticed this for years and years, but love notices everything, and these two lovers were the first to find it and make it a pathway for their conversations. Safely through this chink they would whisper to each other their loving words, and often, when Pyramus was standing on one side of the wall and Thisbe on the other, listening in turn to the sound of each other's breathing, they would say: "You cruel wall, why do you stand in the way of our love? Perhaps it is too much to ask that you should disappear so that we could really meet; but you might at least open a little bit, so that we could kiss each other. All the same we are grateful to you, and admit that it is because of you that our words can reach the ears that love to hear them."

So they would speak, each unfortunately on the wrong side. At nightfall they would say good-bye, and each would press on the wall opposite kisses that could not go through to the other side.

When dawn next day had scattered the stars and the rays of the sun had dried the dew from the grass, they came together again. First in low whispers they complained, and then they decided that in the silence of the night they would try to escape notice and steal out of doors. When they were out of their houses, they would leave the city too, and, so that they should not have to wander about in the open country, they agreed to meet at the tomb of Ninus where they would hide in the shade of a tree. There was a tree there (a very tall mulberry) covered with snow-white fruit, near an icy-cold fountain. This idea pleased them very much, and daylight seemed to them to last a long time. But finally the sun plunged into the waves, and out of the waves came night.

In the darkness Thisbe cautiously swung back the door on its hinges and went out. None of her people saw her and, covering her face with a veil, she came to the tomb and sat down under the tree. Her love gave her courage.

Then suddenly a lioness appeared. She had just been killing cattle and her mouth was all smeared with blood. Now she had come to quench her thirst in the water of the spring near the tree. Far off in the moonlight Babylonian Thisbe saw the lioness, and fled trembling into a dark cave, but as she fled her veil slipped from her neck and she left it behind.

The savage lioness drank deeply to quench her thirst and, on her way back to the forest, happened to find, not Thisbe herself, but the dainty scarf she had left behind her. This she tore up with her bloody jaws.

Pyramus arrived a little later and saw deeply marked in the sand what he knew were the footprints of a wild beast. His face went white, and then, when he found the clothes too, all stained with blood, he cried out: "One night will make an end of two lovers. Of us two she was the one who ought to have lived longest. It is I who was to blame. You poor thing, it is I who have destroyed you, because I asked you to come to such a dangerous place by night and did not arrive there first. O you lions who live among these rocks, tear my body to pieces, bite up my wicked flesh in your terrible jaws! But only cowards pray for death."

Then he picked up Thisbe's scarf and took it with him to the shade of the tree where they had planned to meet. First he wept over the scarf which he knew so well, and kissed it. Then he said to it: "Now you must drink my blood too," and immediately plunged the sword which he carried into his side, and drew it out, dying, from the hot wound. As he lay prostrate on the ground the blood spurted up high into the air, just as when, through a defect in the lead, a pipe bursts and through the little hole the water shoots out hissing in a stream, and leaps up into the air. The fruit on the tree was sprayed with his blood and turned black. The roots too were soaked, and as a result gave a purple color to the hanging berries.

And now, still frightened, but frightened too of missing her lover, Thisbe returned and looked about everywhere for him, anxious to tell him about the great danger which she had escaped. She recognized the surroundings and the shape of the tree which she knew, but the changed color of the fruit made her uncertain. She wondered whether this was really the tree or not, and while she was hesitating she saw someone's limbs twitching on the bloody ground. She took a pace backwards, her face turned more white than boxwood, and she shuddered as the sea shivers when a little breeze just strokes its surface. Soon she recognized the body of her love, and then she violently struck herself on her guiltless arms, tore her hair, embraced his body, filling his wounds with tears, mingling her weeping with his blood. She pressed kisses on his cold face and cried out: "O Pyramus, what is it that has taken you from me? Pyramus, answer me! It is your dearest Thisbe calling to you. Listen to me! Raise up your drooping head!"

At the sound of Thisbe's name, Pyramus lifted up his eyes which were already heavy with death, and, when he had seen her, he shut them again.

Thisbe then recognized her own veil and saw that the ivory sheath had no sword in it. "So it was your own hand, unhappy one, and your love for me which killed you? I, too, have a hand brave enough for this, and I love you too. My love will give me strength to make the wound. I shall go with you, and people will say that I was not only the cause but also the companion of your death. Only death could have parted you from me, and now not even death shall have the power to do so. And you, our unhappy parents, mine and his, I pray you in the name of both of us that you will not refuse that we, joined together by fixed love and by our last hours, should be buried together in the same tomb. I pray too, that this tree which now covers with its boughs the sad body of one of us and will soon cover mine as well, I pray that in memory of our blood it may always keep the color in its fruit and have berries suitable for mourning and be a memorial to both of our deaths."

As she spoke, she fitted the point of the sword, still warm from his blood, under her breast and fell forward on it. But both the gods and her parents were touched by her prayers. The color of the mulberry, when ripe, is dark red: and the ashes of Pyramus and Thisbe rest in the same urn.

Cadmus

CADMUS was a prince of Tyre. Jupiter had fallen in love with his sister, Europa, had changed himself into a bull and had carried the girl away to the fields of Crete. But her father, Agenor, with no idea of what had happened, ordered Cadmus to look for the lost girl throughout the world, and gave him the punishment of exile, if he failed to find her. In one way this was a fair thing to do: in another way it was unfair, since nobody could keep track of all Jupiter's secret loves.

So Cadmus wandered all over the world and became an exile, keeping away from his own country where his father's anger would await him. Finally he visited the oracle of Phoebus and asked whether there was any land in which he could settle down. Phoebus gave him this reply: "In a desert place you will meet a cow, one that has never had a yoke on her neck or drawn a hooked plow. Follow her as she goes and in the place where she first lies down on the grass, there you must found your city, and you must call the place Boeotia, or Cowland."

Almost as soon as Cadmus had come down from the cave where the oracle was, he saw a young cow, with no one looking after her, walking slowly along, and with no mark on her to show that she had ever been used for plowing or belonged to anybody. He walked carefully on after her, and, as he went, he silently gave thanks to Phoebus for his guidance.

The cow went across the fords of the river Cephisus and through the fields of Panope. Then she stood still and, lifting up her head, which was very beautiful with its long horns, she filled the air all round with her lowings. Then she gave a look back at Cadmus and his men who were following her, and sank down on the ground, letting her flanks rest in the cool grass. Cadmus gave thanks to the gods, kissed this foreign earth and greeted the mountains and fields that he had never seen before.

The next thing was to make a sacrifice to Jupiter, and he ordered his men to go and find a spring of living water for the libations. There was an ancient forest nearby which had never been touched by the axe, and in the middle of it was a cave all overgrown with bushes and bending twigs. Stones fitted together there formed a low arch out of which welled a stream of water, and, hidden inside the cave, was a serpent sacred to Mars with a wonderful golden crest. Its eyes sparkled with fire: all its body was swollen with poison. It had three tongues which flickered out and three rows of teeth.

As soon as Cadmus's men came, unluckily for them, to this wood, they let down their buckets with a splash into the water, and immediately, out of the depths of the cave the blue serpent stretched out its head and made a terrible hissing. The buckets dropped from their hands, the blood left their bodies, and a sudden trembling came over their limbs. As for the serpent, it gathered itself up with its scaly coils into rolling circles; with a quick movement it arched itself up and, with more than half of its body upright in the air, it looked right down on the trees. It was as big, if you could have seen the whole of it, as the constellation in the sky which is called the Serpent, and is placed between the Great Bear and the Little Bear. Without a second's delay it seized upon Cadmus's men, and it made no difference whether they were getting their swords ready to fight or were thinking of running away or were too terrified to do either. Some of them it killed with its teeth, some by crushing them in its long coils, some by its deadly poisonous breath.

By the time that the sun had reached its full height and the shadows were at their smallest, Cadmus began to wonder why his men were being so long, and he set out to look for them. He carried a lion-skin shield, and his weapons were a shining iron-pointed spear and a javelin. His own stout heart was worth more than any weapon.

When he entered the wood he saw the dead bodies and, sprawling over them in triumph, the huge body of their destroyer, who now with its bloody tongue was licking their grim wounds. "My faithful friends," Cadmus said, "I shall either avenge your death or share in it."

As he spoke he lifted up in his right hand a great stone. It was a huge stone and he threw it with a huge effort; but, though high walls with their towers would have been

knocked down by its force, the serpent remained without a wound. Its scales, like a breastplate, and its hard dark skin protected it against the blow. However, the skin was not too hard for Cadmus's javelin, which fixed firmly and stuck in the middle of the serpent's coiling muscular back, with the iron head going right down into the flesh. Infuriated with pain, the animal twisted its head back, examined its wounds, and bit at the shaft of the javelin that was stuck in it. Tugging violently at it, it managed, when it had loosened it all round, to tear it out; but the point was still stuck in its backbone. Now indeed it had reason to be more savage than ever before. Great veins swelled up on its throat; a white foam shone round its grisly open jaws; its scales made a terrible rustling sound on the earth; a black breath, like that which comes from the mouth of Styx, made the air filthy and tainted. At one moment it coiled itself up into huge folds; the next moment it shot up into the air erect and high as a tree; then it surged forward in a huge wave, like a flooded river, battering down with its breast the trees that stood in its path.

Cadmus retreated a little, holding his lion-skin shield in front of him, and jabbing with his spear point at the open jaws that were always threatening him. The beast became all the more enraged, as it bit uselessly on the hard iron, fixing its teeth into the point of the spear. Soon blood began to fall from the poisonous roof of its mouth and to stain the green grass around. But the wound was not a serious one, because the serpent kept backing away and withdrawing its wounded neck, and so never gave Cadmus a chance to thrust his blow home. Finally, however, he fixed the spear firmly in the beast's throat and pressed on hard till he had driven it back against an oak tree. There the spear went right through both the neck and the tree. The tree bent down beneath its weight and the trunk groaned as, in its death agony, the serpent lashed it with its tail.

Then, while Cadmus was standing looking at the enormous size of his defeated enemy, he suddenly heard a voice. He had no idea where it came from, but he heard it saying: "Son of Agenor, why are you looking at this dead serpent? A time will come when *you* will be turned into a serpent, and people will be looking at *you*." On hearing these words he stood in terror for some time, with pale face and uneasy mind. Cold fear made his hair stand on end.

Then suddenly Pallas, his patron goddess, appeared, gliding down to him through the upper air. She told him to plow up the land and sow the dragon's teeth in it, and they would grow up to be his people. He obeyed her, plowing long furrows as he pressed his plow into the earth. He took the teeth, which were to be the seeds of men, as he had been told, and scattered them. Then, incredible as it may seem, the edges of the furrows began to show signs of movement. First there sprang up out of the ground the points of spears, then helmets with bright-colored nodding crests. Then above the surface there began to show shoulders and breasts and arms heavy with their weapons. So out of the earth came a whole crop of warriors with their shields.

Cadmus was terrified at finding that he had new enemies to deal with, and he was beginning to take up his arms when one of the earth-born people cried out to him:

"Leave your arms alone! This is a war among ourselves. Do not join in it." He then struck down with his stout sword, fighting hand to hand, one of his earth-born brothers, and wash himself struck down by a javelin thrown at him from long range. Yet the man who killed him lived no longer himself, immediately giving up the life which he had only just received. In the same way the whole crowd of them fought bitterly, each man killing his neighbor, brothers only for a very short time. Soon all these young men, whose life had been so short, were dying in agony on their mother earth, all warm with their blood. Only five were left. One of these was called Echion, and at the command of Pallas, he threw down his weapons on the ground and proposed peace to his brothers. The fighting was over and Cadmus had these five men for his companions in founding the city which had been promised him by the oracle of Phoebus.

Actaeon

ONE might have thought now that Cadmus was really happy. His city of Thebes was built. He was given the daughter of Venus and Mars, Harmonia, to be his wife. He had four daughters who were called Ino, Agave, Autonoe and Semele. They in turn had children who began to grow up to be men and women. So one would certainly have expected Cadmus and Harmonia to be happy. However, one should always wait for the end, and no one can be called happy until he is dead and buried.

The first reason for sadness that came on Cadmus and Harmonia in the midst of all this good fortune was the fate of their grandson Actaeon, the son of Autonoe. Deer's horns grew on his head and his own hounds drank up their master's blood. And if you think about the story you will see that this was just because of bad luck, not because he did anything wrong. There is nothing wrong in just making a mistake.

Actaeon had been hunting on a mountain, and all the ground was stained with the blood of the wild animals which he had killed. It was midday and the sun stood high up in the sky, making all the shadows short. Young Actaeon with gentle words called to his hunting companions as they strayed through the bushes and thickets: "My friends, all our nets and spears are wet with blood. We have done well enough today. When tomorrow's dawn brings back the light in her shining chariot, then we will start our hunting again. Now Phoebus is halfway across the sky and his rays seem to split the ground. Let us rest now and take up our knotted nets." His companions did as they were told and gave up their work.

There was a valley in this forest, all overgrown with pine trees and sharp-pointed cypresses. It was called Gargaphie and was sacred to the huntress goddess Diana. At the far end of the valley there was a shady cave, not specially constructed but made by nature to look as though it was a work of art; for there was a natural arch there made out of the original rock. From one side came the noise of a shining fountain which bubbled up from the ground and formed a pool with grassy banks. And in this pool Diana, when she was tired from hunting, used to bathe her virgin limbs in the bright water.

This day, too, she had come there. To the nymph who acted as her armor-bearer she gave her javelin, her quiver and her unstrung bow to hold. Another nymph held over her arm the dress which the goddess took off. Two others removed her sandals. Another, with her own hair streaming behind her, tied in a knot the hair that fell over the goddess's shoulders, and other nymphs fetched water in their ewers for the goddess's bath.

At this moment, just when Diana was bathing in her usual pool, Cadmus's grandson, having stopped hunting for the day, came wandering with no special purpose through the unknown woods and arrived at Diana's sacred grove. It was fate that brought him there.

As soon as he peered into the cave, all shining with the fountain spray, the naked nymphs, seeing a man, beat their breasts and filled all the grove with their startled cries. They crowded round Diana and tried to shield her with their own bodies, but the goddess was taller than any of them and stood out head and shoulders above the rest. As she stood there naked and in view, she blushed the color of the clouds when the sun strikes slanting across them, red as the dawn. With the nymphs all around her, she turned aside, looking behind her as though for her arrows. But she had no weapons by her except the water, and, taking up some of this, she dashed it into the young man's face and poured the avenging stream over his hair. Then she spoke words foretelling the fate that would soon come upon him. "Now," she said, "tell, if you can tell, how you have seen me naked!"

This was all she said, but, as she spoke, she made stag's horns grow out of his head which she had splashed with the water; she lengthened out his neck and made his ears pointed; instead of hands she gave him hooves; she changed his arms into long legs, and covered his body with a spotted hide. She also made him frightened. The hero Actaeon began to run away, and, while doing so, was astonished to find that he was running so fast. But when he came to a pool and saw his changed face and his horns in the water, he tried to say, "O how unhappy I am," but found that he could not pronounce the words. He groaned (this was the only way he could speak at all). Tears ran down his cheeks, though they were not really his cheeks. Only his mind and his feelings remained unchanged. What was he to do? Should he go back home to the royal palace or should he hide in the woods? He felt ashamed to go home, but frightened to stay where he was.

While he stood wondering what to do, his hounds saw him. First came Blackfoot and keen-scented Trailer, baying to the others. Trailer was a Cretan hound, Blackfoot came from Sparta. Then the others came rushing up, faster than the wind—Greedy and Gazelle, and Hill-treader, all dogs from Arcadia, strong Fawn-slayer, Hunter and Hurricane, swift Flyer and keen-scented Chaser. There were Forester, who had just been wounded by a wild boar, Glen, who was half a wolf, and more than twenty other strong fierce baying hounds. The whole pack of them, eager for the chase, came rushing over the rocks and broken ground, darting through the thickets and appearing, as it were, from nowhere.

Actaeon found himself being chased over the very ground where he had often chased animals himself. He was running away from his own hounds, which he had trained himself, and longed to cry out: "I am Actaeon. You must recognize me. I am your own master." But, however much he wanted to, he was unable to speak.

A hound called Soot was the first one to fix teeth in his back; then came Barker, and then Mountaineer leaped on to his shoulder and hung on. These had started later than the others but had taken a short cut through the mountains and so arrived first. While they held their master fast, the rest of the pack came up and buried their fangs in his body. Soon there was no room left on his skin for further wounds. He groaned aloud, making a sound which, while it was not exactly human, was not the sound that an ordinary stag would make. He filled all the mountain ridges that he knew so well with his sad cries, and, falling on his knees, like someone begging for a favor, he looked round in silence on his persecutors, turning his face to them, as though he were stretching out his arms to ask for mercy.

But his young friends, knowing nothing of the real facts, kept on shouting to the swift hounds, as they usually did, and urging them on to the kill. They all looked round for Actaeon and were always shouting out his name, imagining that he was not there. At the sound of his name, the stag turned his head towards them, but they just said that it was a pity that Actaeon was not there, that he must have been too lazy to come and see this fine sight of the animal brought to bay. Indeed he might well wish that he was not there, but he was. He might well wish to be watching his hounds and not feeling their savage teeth. But as it was they were all about him, burying their muzzles in his flesh, and tearing their own master to pieces in the belief that it was a stag that they were killing. Not till wound had followed wound, and his life was over, was the anger of Diana, the archer goddess, appeased.

Pentheus

ANOTHER of Cadmus's grandsons, Pentheus, came to a sad end, though he deserved his fate more than Actaeon did. Pentheus was the son of Echion, the earthborn soldier who had helped Cadmus to build Thebes, and of Agave, the daughter of Cadmus and Harmonia. In Cadmus's old age Pentheus became the ruler of Thebes and he met his death by offending the new god Bacchus, who was, in a way, his own cousin, since he was the child of Jupiter and of Pentheus's aunt Semele.

Bacchus, the god of wine, had been brought up secretly, since Juno, the wife of Jupiter, hated him. First he was worshiped in the East but later came back into Greece with his band of revelers. Women in particular joined in the adoration of the new god, dancing and singing in his honor along the mountains. But there were some men, Pentheus among them, who tried to put down the new religion. These men all came to bad ends.

In Thebes there was a famous blind prophet called Tiresias. Most people honored him, but Pentheus, who was apt to scoff at holy things, laughed at the old man's prophecies and was rude to him about his blindness. The prophet shook his head in disapproval and his white locks swung as he shook it. "How lucky you would be," he said to Pentheus, "if you too were blind so that you could never watch the worship of Bacchus. For the day will come— indeed I know that it is almost here—when the new god, Bacchus, the son of Semele, will come to this country. And unless you honor him and build temples to him, you will be torn into a thousand pieces, your body will be scattered far and wide, and your blood will stain the forests and the hands of your mother and her sisters. This is sure to happen, for I know that you will not give the god the honor he deserves. Then you will be sorry and say that, blind as I am, I have seen far too well."

Pentheus pushed Tiresias away out of his house while he was speaking, but his words came true, and what he had foretold actually took place.

Bacchus did arrive and soon all the country was full of shouting and revelry. Everyone rushed out of the city, men and women, old and young, rich and poor, to join in the new religion. They danced and sang about the mountains, carrying wands tipped with fir cones, wearing garlands of ivy and the skins of fawns. To those who were not worshipers they might seem like mad people, but they felt themselves filled with the god, and, when they smote the ground with their wands, streams of milk came out from the rocks.

Pentheus alone was indignant. "Children of the serpent's teeth," he cried out, "children of Mars, what is this crazy madness? Are you overcome just by the noise of cymbals clashing together or of those long crooked horns, or by a set of magic tricks, and women howling out, vulgar crowds, drunkenness and empty dreams? You who were never frightened by the noise of trumpets in war or the thought of drawn swords and real fighting! And you, old men who with my grandfather came over the sea to found this city, I am surprised at you. Will you allow Thebes to be captured by an unarmed boy, who has no spears or horsemen and whose only weapons are perfumed hair, soft garlands and clothes richly woven with purple and gold? Let me deal with him at once by myself. I shall soon force him to admit that he made up the name of his father and that his new religion is nothing but trickery. Go at once, my slaves, and bring this impostor back in chains! Let there be no hanging back and no laziness in obeying my orders!"

His grandfather Cadmus, and all the elders, urged him not to speak like this, but to be more wise. Their words however had no effect on him. Indeed the more good advice they gave him, the more stubborn he became. All their efforts to control him merely did harm.

Soon the slaves came back, covered with blood and bringing with them a young man with his hands tied behind him. "Where is Bacchus?" Pentheus asked, and they replied, "We could not find him, but we have seized this man who is a companion of his and a priest of his religion."

Pentheus, with eyes made terrible with anger, glanced at the prisoner. He was hardly able to control himself from putting him to death at once. "You are soon going to die," he shouted at him, "and be an example to others by your death. But first tell me your name and your family and where you come from and why you are busying yourself with this new religion."

The young man, showing no sign of fear, replied: "My name is Acoetes. I come from Maeonia. My parents were humble people. My father could not leave me any fields to plow with strong oxen, or any woolly sheep or cattle. He was a poor man himself and used to earn his living by catching fish with a line and hooks and rods. He had no property apart from his skill, and when he died he could leave me nothing but the open sea. This is the only thing that I can say I got from my father. However, so as not to be always fixed to the same bit of rocky shore, I soon began to learn how to steer a ship and all about the stars used in navigation, about the various winds and about the best harbors and anchorages. So I took to the sea and once, when I was on my way to Delos, I was driven off my course and put in, using the oars, to the island of Chios. There we jumped out of the boat and landed on the wet sand. We spent the night there and, as soon as dawn grew red, I told my men to fetch fresh water and showed them the path that went to the spring. I myself went up a small hill to see what the wind was doing. Then I called to my men and started back to the ship. 'Here we are, and see what we have got,' shouted back Opheltes, one of the sailors, and brought up to me what he thought was a useful piece of booty which he had come across in an empty field. It was a young boy with beauty like a girl's beauty. This boy looked as though he was drowsy with wine. He

seemed to stagger as he walked and could hardly keep step
with those who were leading him. I looked carefully at his
clothes and his face and his way of walking. There was
nothing in any of these which seemed to me mortal. I realized this at once and I said to my men: 'Exactly what sort
of divinity there is in this body I do not know, but in this
body there certainly is divinity.' Then I turned to the boy
and said, 'Whoever you may be, I pray you to look favor-
ably on us and help us. And please forgive these men who
have captured you.'

" 'There is no need to pray for us,' said Dictys. He was
the best of all the men at climbing to the topmost yard and
sliding down to deck again on a firmly gripped rope. The
others agreed with him, Libys and yellow-haired Melan-
thus the lookout man, Alcimedon and Epopeus who con-
trolled the rowers' rate of stroke and used to urge them on
with his voice. So did all the rest, so blind they were in
their desire to make profit out of their prize.

" 'Then I, in any case,' I said, 'shall refuse to allow the
ship to be used for such an evil purpose. And here I have
authority.'

"I tried to stop them coming on board, but Lycabas, one
of the roughest of the whole crew, a man who had been
exiled for murder, broke into a rage, seized hold of my
throat with his great hands and would have thrown me
overboard, if I had not, in my terror, managed to cling on
to a rope. The other godless men were all supporting him,
when at last Bacchus (for this boy was Bacchus himself)
seemed to come to his senses, as though all the shouting
had woken him up from a drowsy drunkenness. 'What are

you doing?' he said. 'Why are you shouting out? Tell me, sailors, how I came here, and where are you taking me.'

" 'Don't be frightened,' Proteus replied. 'Tell us where you want to go and we will put you down at whatever harbor you choose.'

" 'Then,' said Bacchus, 'take me to Naxos. My home is there, and there you shall have a friendly welcome.'

"Then these deceitful men swore by the sea, and by all the gods that they would do as he had asked, and they told me to get the bright-painted ship under sail.

"Naxos was on the right, and, as I was setting course to the right, Opheltes shouted out, 'What are you doing, you madman? We want to go to the left.' Others frowned and winked at me or whispered in my ear, threatening me.

"I was simply amazed. 'Let someone else take the helm then,' I said. 'I refuse to be used to help your wicked treachery.'

"Then they were all against me and turned on me with angry mutterings. Aethalion said: 'You need not suppose that you are the only one who can steer a boat,' and he came and took my place at the helm, turning away from Naxos and making in the opposite direction.

"Then the god, playing with them and making them think that he had only just discovered their treachery, stared out over the sea from the hooked stern and, looking as though he was crying, said: 'O sailors, this is not the shore you promised me. This is not the land where I wanted to be. How have I deserved this from you? Surely you cannot be proud of what you are doing, all of you against one, men against a little boy!'

"As for me I was in tears already, but my wicked men laughed at my tears and struck the water eagerly with their oars, anxious to make land where they could sell their prisoner as a slave.

"Now I swear to you by Bacchus himself (and there is no god more near to you at this moment than he is) that I am telling a true story, incredible as it may seem. Suddenly the ship stuck still in the water, just as if it were in dry dock. The sailors, in amazement, redoubled the strokes of their oars. Then they began to shake out every sail, hoping that with sails and oars together the ship might move. But ivy began to grow round the oars and prevent their motion. Ivy began to climb up the mast, twining and hanging in folds and spreading its clusters of black berries against the white of the sails. The god himself appeared with a crown of leaves and clustering berries on his forehead and in his hand was an ivy wand. Around him there appeared the shapes of tigers and lynxes: at his feet seemed to be lying the fierce bodies of spotted leopards.

"The men, in madness or in terror, jumped overboard. First I noticed that Medon's body had begun to turn black and that his backbone was bending into a regular curve. Lycabas saw this too and was starting to say, 'O Medon, you are turning into some strange animal,' but, as he was speaking, his own jaws expanded sideways, his nose became hooked, his skin hardened and began to be covered with scales. Libys, while he was still tugging at ivy-wreathed oars, suddenly saw his hands shrinking into things that were not hands at all, but fins. Another sailor, as he tried to pull on one of the twisted ropes, found that

34

his arms had disappeared and plunged backwards into the sea without limbs. At the end of his body was a tail curved like the horns of the moon.

"So they leaped about on every side in the water, scattering the spray, plunging under the surface and coming up again, playing together like a troupe of dancers, rolling their bodies sportively in the waves, breathing in the sea through their wide nostrils and blowing it out again.

"Out of twenty men (which was the number of the crew) I was the only survivor. I stood there trembling and cold with fear, hardly conscious of myself. But the god strengthened me. 'Do not be afraid,' he said. 'Hold on the course for Naxos.'

"When we arrived there I joined the religion of Bacchus and now I am one of his worshipers."

Pentheus heard the story and said: "If you think that this long idle tale will soften my anger, you are mistaken. Quickly, slaves, take this man away. Make him suffer every torture, and so send his body to death in the night of Styx."

Immediately Acoetes, who had told the story, was dragged out and shut up behind strong prison walls. But while his executioners were preparing the cruel instruments of torture—red-hot irons and racks—suddenly the prison doors flew open of their own accord, the chains fell of their own accord from the prisoner's arms, and the prisoner was gone.

In spite of this Pentheus remained obstinate. This time he did not send messengers, but went himself to Mount Cithaeron, which was the special place outside Thebes where Bacchus was worshiped and which was loud with the singing and shouting of his worshipers. As he heard the whole air full of the shouting and the crying, Pentheus's anger boiled up all the more in him. It had the effect on him that the sound of trumpets has on a spirited war horse.

About halfway up the mountain there is an open space, in full view from all sides, with woods around it. Here Pentheus was spying with his unclean eyes on the sacred mysteries of the new religion. His mother, Agave, was the first to see him. She first was driven mad and rushed upon her son, hurling at him her wand of ivy. "Look, sisters," she cried out, "look at this huge wild boar prowling about in our field. I want to be the one to kill him."

The whole rout of women rushed down upon the one man. All gathered round him and pursued him, frightened now, as he well might be, and speaking in quite a different tone from that one which he had used before. Now he was ready to condemn himself and to admit that he had been wrong. But they tore at his body from all sides. Wounded as he was, he cried out to his aunt, Autonoe, "O, help me, aunt! Remember Actaeon, and have pity on me!"

But she, driven out of her mind, did not even remember who Actaeon was. As Pentheus stretched out his arm to her, she seized it and, with the strength of madness, tore it off. Ino, in the same rage, tore off the other arm. Now the wretched man had no arms to stretch out for pity to his mother. "O Mother," he said, "look!" and he turned towards her the stumps where his arms had been. Agave, tossing her head with its streaming hair, and howling at the sight of him, tore off his head and, holding it in her fingers which were streaming with blood, she shouted out: "Look, my friends and sisters! See what I have done and see my triumph!"

Then like the wind after the first autumn frosts quickly strips the insecure leaves from high trees, so was the body of Pentheus torn to pieces and scattered by terrible and ignorant hands. Agave, with her sisters, returned to Thebes and, holding the head of Pentheus, came, still mad, to her father Cadmus and boasted to him of how she had killed the wild boar. Cadmus wept to see her and to see his grandson's fate. Very gradually he persuaded her, as her madness began to subside, that what she held in her hands was not a boar's head, but the head of her own son, who had refused to honor the new god. With such a fate to warn them, the Thebans in great numbers adopted the new religion, burned incense and sacrificed before the altars of Bacchus.

Ino

THE death of Pentheus was not the last of the misfortunes which fell upon the house of Cadmus. Juno still hated the whole family and she now turned her hatred against Cadmus's daughter Ino, who was proud of her children, proud of her husband Athamas, and particularly proud of the new god, Bacchus, whom, after his mother's death, she had helped to bring up.

Juno looked on her with hatred and envy. She remembered how Bacchus, the child of her own husband by another woman, had been able to change the sailors into dolphins and make Agave kill her own son. "And now," she said to herself, "is there nothing I can do except lament and be jealous? Am I not also powerful? Bacchus has shown me what to do. He has shown only too clearly, by the killing of Pentheus, how strong madness can be. Why should not Ino also be driven mad?"

So she decided to go down to the lower world of the ghosts and seek help from the Furies there.

There is a road going downhill and shaded by deathly

yew trees. It leads down in utter silence to the kingdom below the earth. There the sluggish stream of the Styx breathes out its damp mists, and on this road the ghosts of those who have just died go down to their habitations. They come to a wide dreary plain, palely lit and icy cold; and there the shades look for the road that leads to the infernal city and the palace of black Pluto, the King of the Dead. This city has a thousand entrances and gates open on every side. As the sea receives all the rivers of the earth, so this place receives all the dead souls. It is big enough to hold whole nations, and when crowds enter it they are unnoticed. Here the thin bloodless ghosts, without flesh or bones, wander to and fro. Some flit about the open squares, some spend their time in the palace of the King of the underworld, some occupy themselves in ways that are an imitation of the life they used to have on earth.

So great was her rage and hatred that Juno left her home in heaven and came down to this dreadful place. As she stepped on to the threshold, it groaned beneath the weight of her holy body, and the three-headed watchdog, Cerberus, raised his heads and barked through his three jaws. Juno called for the Furies, who were children of Night, terrible and implacable goddesses. They sat in front of the closed adamantine prison gates of Hell, and as they sat there, they combed back from their heads the black snakes which were their hair. They rose to their feet when they recognized Juno through the dark mist.

This prison house is called the Place of Wickedness, and here the great sinners are punished. The giant Tityus was here, with his huge body stretched over nine acres. Vultures continually devoured his flesh, which continually grew again. He at one time had offered violence to Latona, the mother of Phoebus and of Diana. There also was Tantalus, who had deceived the gods. He was in continual thirst, with water just at his lips but never reaching them, and with fruit trees hanging round his head but always disappearing when he stretched out his hands to the fruit. Then there was Sisyphus, whose punishment was forever to roll a huge rock to the top of a hill. Whenever he had pushed the rock to the summit it always rolled back again to the plain and his task had to be begun anew. Ixion, who had dared to attack Juno herself, was whirled for ever on a wheel. There also were the fifty Belides, daughters of a king of Egypt, who had murdered their husbands. They were condemned to fetch water in pitchers from one place to another, but the task was never done, as the water always ran from the pitchers on the way.

On all these criminals, and especially on Ixion, Juno looked with fierce eyes. Then she looked at Sisyphus, who had been the brother of Ino's husband Athamas. "Why should this brother," she said, "have to suffer endless torture, while Athamas and his wife, who despise me, live happily in a rich palace?"

She then told the Furies why she had come and what she wanted—which was the complete ruin of the house of Cadmus and that Athamas should be driven mad. When she had finished, the Fury Tisiphone shook her grey tangled hair and brushed back the snakes that swarmed over her forehead. "There is no need," she said, "for you to say more. What you want will be done. Now leave this loveless kingdom and go back to the purer air of heaven."

Pleased with her success, Juno returned and, as she entered Heaven, Iris, the goddess of the rainbow, sprinkled water over her to purify her.

Meanwhile the terrible Tisiphone hurriedly seized hold of a torch that had been drenched in blood. She put on a dress, wet also with blood, and knotted round her waist a writhing snake. Then she left the lower world and with her went Grief and Terror and Madness with quivering lips. She took her stand in the doorway of the house of Athamas and they say that the very doorposts trembled at her presence and turned pale. The sun fled from the sky. At the awful sight both Ino and Athamas were overwhelmed with terror and tried to run away. But the terrible Fury stood in the entrance and stopped them escaping. She stretched out her arms which were covered with writhing vipers and shook out her hair which was hissing with snakes that fell in coils over her breast and shoulders, spitting out poison with their flickering tongues. Two of these snakes she plucked out of her hair and flung at Athamas and at Ino. They glided over their bodies, not biting them, but distilling their terrible poison into their minds. Then the Fury seized up her torch and whirled it round her head till it burst into a roaring flame. Her task was done and her victory complete. She returned to Hell and undid the serpents which had girdled her dress.

Immediately Athamas, now raving mad, shouted out in the middle of his palace. "Come, my friends, spread out the nets here in this forest! I have just seen a lioness with her two cubs." Then, quite out of his wits, he rushed after his wife as though she were a wild beast. He snatched from her arms his little son Learchus who was smiling at him and stretching out his hands to him, and dashed the baby to the ground. Ino, herself now mad, either because of the Fury or because of what her husband had done, gave a great cry and seized up her little child, Melicertes, in her bare arms. With her hair streaming behind her and shouting out the name of Bacchus, she fled from the house. Juno heard her cry and laughed. "Your foster child, Bacchus," she said, "is not going to be of any help to you now."

There was a cliff overhanging the sea. Its base had been all hollowed out by the waves, so that the water surged right underneath it. Its top stood high and sharp over the deep sea. Ino in her madness climbed to the very summit and, with no fear, threw herself and her child right out into the sea. The water foamed and whitened in the place where she fell.

Venus, however, pitied the undeserved suffering of her granddaughter and prayed to her uncle Neptune, the god of the sea: "O Neptune, you who rule the waters, you whose power is second only to Jupiter, my request is a big one, but please grant it. Have pity on these friends of mine! The sea owes me something, since in the depths of the sea I was born from the foam, and my Greek name, Aphrodite, means this."

Neptune heard her prayer and changed Ino and her child into divine creatures. The little boy became a sea god, Palaemon, and his mother a goddess, Lencothoe.

Cadmus, however, had no means of knowing that his daughter and his grandson had been changed into gods of the sea. He was overcome by grief at all the terrible things that had happened to his family, and he left the city which he had founded, as if it was the bad luck of the place, and not his own, which was hanging over him. With his wife he fled away and came in the end to the borders of Illyria. Here, still grieving over all their sorrows, they were discussing all the misfortunes which had come upon their family. Cadmus was saying, "I wonder whether the serpent, which I killed with my spear and whose teeth bore a crop of men, was a sacred serpent. If it is perhaps the death of this serpent that the gods have been avenging on my family, then I pray that I may turn into a serpent myself and have a long snaky body stretched out on the ground."

As he was speaking, this was exactly what did begin to happen to him. He fell down on to his face; his legs joined into one and then lengthened out into a long pointed tail. His arms still remained, and, with tears streaming down what was still his own human face, he stretched his arms out to his wife. "Come to me, my poor wife!" he said, "Come, while there is still something of me left. Touch me, and take my hand, while I have a hand, before I become entirely snake!"

He wanted to go on speaking, but suddenly found that his tongue had become forked, and he could not pronounce the words. Whenever he tried to say something sad, he made a hissing noise. This was the only voice he had.

His wife beat her breast and cried out: "O stay, Cadmus!

44

Come back to yourself! O whatever is happening? Where are your feet and your hands and your shoulders and your face? Oh, now everything is gone. O gods, why will you not turn me into a snake too?"

As she spoke he licked his wife's face and came naturally to her bosom, as though he knew the place, winding himself round her neck in an embrace. All who saw this were terrified; but she stroked the glowing neck of the crested snake, and suddenly there were two snakes there with their coils twined together. Soon they glided away into hiding in a nearby wood. To this day they are not frightened of men, and do not hurt them. They remember what they once were, and are mild gentle snakes.

Baucis and Philemon

MANY stories go to show how enormous, and indeed limitless, is the power of the gods. If they wish anything, then it is immediately accomplished. For example, there is a place in Phrygia, among the mountains, where an oak and a lime tree, with a low wall round them, are growing side by side. I have seen the place myself, and this is the story of it.

Not far away is a huge lake, which was once land with houses and cities and men and women in it, though now it is the home of coots and diving ducks. At the time when it was inhabited, Jupiter himself and Mercury, laying aside his wings and his wand of twisted snakes, took on the appearance of mortals and visited the place. They went to a thousand houses asking for a meal and somewhere to rest, but in all of them the bolts were drawn and no hospitality was offered. There was only one house that would receive them, a poor and humble one, thatched with straw and reeds. In this cottage good old Baucis and her husband Philemon, who was of the same age, had first come to live when they were young and had grown old in it. Their poverty was no burden to them, because they admitted it and bore it with contented minds. In this house there would be no point in looking for masters and servants, since the two old people formed the entire household. Both were servants and both were masters.

When the two gods reached this humble house, and, stooping down, went in through a low door, the old man Philemon pulled forward a bench and invited them to rest their limbs. Baucis hurried up busily and threw a rough covering over the bench. Then she moved aside the warm ashes in the grate, put in leaves and bark and brought to life yesterday's fire by kneeling down and blowing at the ashes through her old lips. When the flame came, she took down from a special place some carefully split kindling wood and dry twigs, which she broke into little pieces and put under the small copper saucepan on the fire. Then she began to chop off the outside leaves of the cabbage which her husband had brought in from his well-watered garden. Philemon meanwhile took a forked stick and lifted down from a smoky beam a side of smoked bacon which had been carefully kept for a long time. He cut a little piece off it and put it into the water to boil. Then they began to pass the time in conversation. So that their guests would be more comfortable, they brought out a couch with legs and frame made of willow wood, and put their mattress on it. They covered the mattress with coverlets that they never used except on special occasions—though these coverlets themselves were made of old cheap stuff, indeed quite the right thing for the old willow bed. On this the gods reclined and Baucis, with her skirt tucked up and with trembling hands, began to lay the table. One of its three legs was too short, so she put a piece of pottery under it to make it level. Then, when it was steady, she wiped it with green mint, and put on it, all in earthenware dishes, some green olives—the fruit sacred to Minerva—some autumn cornel-fruit that had been pickled in wine, endives, radishes, and eggs lightly done in the warm ashes. Then she put on the table a bowl for the wine, also made of earthenware, and beech-wood drinking cups with their insides smeared and polished with yellow wax. Soon the hot dish was ready from the fire, and old Philemon brought out his wine, which was of no great age or quality. Then the dishes were cleared away for the second course, which consisted of nuts and figs and dried dates, plums and sweet-smelling apples in broad baskets and purple grapes just picked from the vine. In the center of the table there was a fine golden honeycomb, and around the table there were cheerful faces, friendliness and ungrudging kindness.

As the meal went on Baucis and Philemon noticed with astonishment that the wine bowl, whenever it was emptied, filled up again of its own accord. They trembled at this miracle and both uttered a prayer. Then they asked pardon for the poor meal which was all that they could afford. One other thing they had, which was a goose. This bird acted as a watchdog for their small cottage, and they decided to kill it for the gods who were their guests. But the goose, flapping about with its wings, was too quick for the two old people and quite wore them out in their efforts to catch it. In the end it seemed to take refuge at the feet of the gods themselves, and the gods told them not to kill it. "We are gods," they said. "As for the wicked people who live in this neighborhood, they shall be punished as they deserve. But you will not share their fate. Now you must leave your house and come with us to the top of the mountain over there."

The two old people did as they were told, and struggled up the long ascent, with walking sticks to help their feeble steps. When they were a bowshot from the top, they looked back and saw that all the land below them was covered in water. Only their own house remained standing. And while they were looking in amazement at the sight and weeping for the fate of their friends, suddenly that old house of theirs, which had been small even for the two of them, turned into a fine temple. Columns rose up in place of the forked sticks which had served for door posts; the straw thatch began to gleam as it turned to gold; on the floor was a marble pavement. Then Jupiter turned to them and spoke, smiling at them: "You good old man, with a wife who is worthy of you, ask me for any gift which you would like to have."

Philemon consulted with Baucis for a few moments and then told the gods what they had decided upon together. "What we ask," he said, "is that we may be your priests and look after your temple. And since we have always lived happily together, let us both die at the same moment, so that I shall never have to see my wife's tomb, nor will she have to attend to my funeral."

The gods granted his prayer. While life was allowed to them, they guarded the temple. And when, worn out with extreme old age, they were standing one day in front of the holy building and talking about their adventures, Baucis suddenly noticed that leaves were growing on Philemon's body and old Philemon noticed that leaves were growing on Baucis too. Bark began to form all over them, but before it reached their faces, they both cried out together and at the same time, "Good-bye, dear wife," and "Good-bye, dear husband." Then the bark closed over them and covered their lips.

To this very day the peasants in this part of the world will show you two trees growing close together with their two trunks wound round each other. I myself have seen the garlands hanging from their boughs and I hung a garland there too, saying, as I did so: "Those who loved the gods have become gods themselves. They worshiped Heaven, and now they must themselves be worshiped."

Daedalus and Icarus

THE wife of Minos, the great king of Crete, was the mother of a strange monster, half bull, half man, who was called the Minotaur. Wishing to hide away this disgrace to his family, Minos employed a famous Greek engineer, Daedalus, to make an enclosure so full of winding difficult passages that the monster could safely be shut up inside and would never find his way out. So Daedalus constructed the famous labyrinth, a maze of such size and with so many deceptive paths that, when the work was over, he himself could hardly find his way back to the main entrance. Inside this labyrinth the Minotaur was shut up, and another story tells how every year, as part of a tribute owed to Minos, boys and girls from Athens were sent to be devoured by the monster. In the end Theseus, the prince of Athens, with the help of Minos's daughter Ariadne, killed the Minotaur and found his way back to safety. But this did not happen for about twenty years.

When Daedalus had finished building the labyrinth, he wished to return to his home in Greece, but he was so useful as an inventor that Minos refused to let him go. So he and his son Icarus were compelled to stay in Crete against their will.

Finally Daedalus, hating his long exile and longing more and more to see his native country from which he was cut off by a long stretch of sea, said to himself: "Though Minos has blocked all my ways of escape by land and by water, there is certainly a way through the sky. That is the way I must go. I admit that he is supreme everywhere else, but he does not rule over the air."

Then he set his mind to work on problems that had never been thought about before, and succeeded in altering the very nature of things. He took feathers and arranged them in a row, beginning with the smallest ones and putting the bigger ones next, so that they looked as though they had grown in the shape of a wing. It was the same method as that by which the country Pan-pipes are made out of reeds of different lengths, fastened together. He tied the feathers together in the middle with twine, and joined them at the base with wax. Then, when they were arranged and fastened, he gave them all a slight bend, so that they looked exactly like the wings of real birds.

While he was working his son Icarus stood and watched him. Sometimes, laughing, he went chasing after a feather that the passing breeze blew away; sometimes he pressed his thumbs into the balls of yellow wax. He did not realize that what he was touching was going to be very dangerous to him, and by his playfulness he kept on interrupting the wonderful work on which his father was engaged.

When Daedalus had given the finishing touches to his

invention, he put on his wings, flapped them up and down and hung poised in the air above the ground. Then he gave his son careful instructions about how to fly. "My advice to you, Icarus," he said, "is to fly at a moderate height. If you go too low, the sea water will weigh the feathers down; if you go too high, the heat of the sun will melt the wax. So you must fly neither too high nor too low. The best thing is to follow me."

While he gave him this advice, he was fitting the strange new wings to his son's shoulders, and, as he did so, tears ran down his aged cheeks and his hands trembled. He kissed his son for what was fated to be the last time, and then, taking to the air, he flew on ahead, anxious for the boy, like a bird which for the first time leads his fledglings out of their high nest into the yielding air. He called out words of encouragement to the boy and taught him to use those fatal wings, constantly looking back, as he flapped his own wings, to see how his son was managing.

On the ground people fishing with long trembling rods, or shepherds leaning on their crooks, or plowmen bent over their plow handles looked up at them in astonishment and came to the conclusion that, since they were flying through the air, they must be gods.

And now they had left several islands—Delos and Paros —behind them. Juno's sacred island of Samos was on the left, and on the right was Calymne, famous for its honey. At this point the boy began to enjoy the daring experience of flight. Longing for the open sky, he forgot to follow his father and climbed higher and higher in the air. As he came nearer to the sun, the scorching rays began to soften the wax that kept the feathers together. The wax melted and Icarus found that he was flapping bare arms which, without their wings, had no hold upon the air. He fell, and the blue sea, which is still called the Icarian Sea, closed over his lips, as he cried out for his father. Unhappy Daedalus, a father no longer, also cried out. "Icarus!" he called, "Where are you? Where have you gone to?" As he was crying out the boy's name, he saw the wings floating on the water. Then he cursed his own invention, found his son's body and buried it. The land is still called after the name of the buried boy.

Perseus

ACRISIUS, King of Argos, had been told by an oracle that he would be killed by his grandson. He therefore determined that his only daughter, Danaë, should never become a mother and he shut her up in a tower of brass under close guard. But with the gods nothing is impossible. She was visited by Jupiter in a shower of gold and by him she became the mother of a baby whom she called Perseus.

Her father, Acrisius, was, as might have been expected, exceedingly angry. He could scarcely execute his own daughter and grandson, but he came as close to doing this as he dared. He set them in the open sea in a little boat with no provisions, and confidently expected that they would either be drowned or would starve to death. However, the gods willed otherwise. The winds and the waves carried the boat to the little island of Seriphus, and here the mother and child were found by a fisherman called Dictys who, in spite of his poverty, treated them kindly and gave them a home.

The king of the island of Seriphus was called Polydectes, and he, as Perseus grew up, became both jealous and frightened of him. He was jealous because Perseus was stronger, more beautiful and more daring than all the other young men of the island. He was frightened because he wished to make Danaë his wife, against her will, and he knew that, so long as Perseus was with her, he would be unable to do this.

He therefore thought of a plan by which he hoped to get rid of Perseus. He invited all the chief men of the island to a great feast, at which it was understood that each of the guests should give the king some valuable present— a horse, or armor, or some rich ornament. He deliberately invited Perseus too, knowing that he was too poor to be able to afford a present. When all the others had given their presents to the king, Perseus, ashamed at having nothing to give, told the king that, though he was too poor to act as the others had done, he would be glad to use what he had, which was only his courage and his skill, in doing the king any service which he thought fit. "Go, then," said Polydectes, "and bring me back the head of the Gorgon, Medusa."

Perseus rose to his feet and left the banqueting hall. He knew that he must either do what the king had ordered or never show his face in Seriphus again; and he knew that the king was planning to destroy him, since no one yet had seen the Gorgons and lived. The Gorgons were three monsters, one of whom, Medusa, with her snaky hair, had once been a human being. They lived at the end of the world and all who set eyes on them were immediately turned into stone.

Perseus might well have despaired, but the gods helped him. Pluto lent him a helmet which had the power of making the wearer invisible. Minerva lent him her bright shining shield. Mercury lent him his winged sandals with which he could fly through the air, and also a curious twisted sword, studded with diamonds and so sharp that it could cut easily through any metal. Minerva also told him the way that he would have to go and some of the dangers which he would have to meet.

So Perseus said good-bye to his mother whom he left in the care of the good fisherman, Dictys. Then he tied his winged sandals to his feet, took his helmet and his sword, and flew over land and sea in the direction of the extreme west.

He came to a country where human beings had never set foot before. The only inhabitants were three old unmarried hags, the daughters of Phorkys and sisters of the Gorgons. They had one eye and one tooth between the three of them, and would make use of them in turn.

Perseus approached them wearing the helmet that made him invisible, and, while one of the old creatures was passing the eye to another, he snatched it from her hand and refused to give it back unless they told him where their sisters, the Gorgons, lived.

Much against their will, and with quavering lips, they told him the way, and again Perseus traveled far through unexplored countries, wildernesses, shaggy woods and sharp bristling rocks, till he came to the country where the Gorgons were. He soon knew that he was in the right place, because all over the fields and roads he saw figures of men and animals which had been turned to stone by one look from Medusa's eyes.

Soon he found in a rocky place the three Gorgons asleep, with their long wings folded about them. He approached them invisibly, and took great care not to look directly at Medusa. Instead he only looked at the reflection of her face and snaky hair in the shield which he carried. Then while sleep held both her and the snakes that coiled about her face, with one blow of his sharp sword he cut the head from the neck, and swift as an arrow, too swift for pursuit, sped away on the pathways of the air.

He put the head, still bleeding, into a bag which he had brought for this purpose. From the first drop of blood that fell on the rocky ground there sprang up a wonderful creature, the winged horse, Pegasus. This beautiful and spirited animal flew through the air to Mount Helicon, where the Muses live, and became their favorite and their pet.

Meanwhile Perseus, on his rushing wings, sped through the light air, carrying the Gorgon's head. As he flew over the sands of Libya, more drops of blood fell to the ground. As they sank into the earth they came to life in the form of snakes, which is why the country of Libya is still infested with these creatures.

And now Perseus was tossed about by discordant winds and storms, driven now here, now there, like a grey cloud. Looking down from his great height he saw the lands beneath and flew over the whole surface of the world. Up to the cold north he was swept and back again to the burning south; often the storms bore him to the sunset and often towards the east. Finally, as night was falling and as he feared to trust himself to the darkness, he landed in the land of Hesperia, the kingdom of the giant Atlas, and asked to be allowed to rest until Dawn rose on the next day.

Atlas was far the most enormous of all creatures in human form. He ruled over the edge of the world where, at sunset, the sun's tired horses plunge into the gleaming sea. In his gardens there was a tree with golden leaves covering branches of gold and golden apples. Perseus came to Atlas and said: "Sir, I beg leave to rest here. If high birth means anything to you, then let me inform you that my father is Jupiter. Or if you are interested in famous deeds, then I think you will be interested in what I have done. I ask you, therefore, for your hospitality."

Atlas, however, remembered an old oracle which had told him that one day a child of Jupiter would come and steal his golden apples, and for this reason he had built huge walls round his orchard, had put a great dragon there to guard the fruit, and refused to allow strangers in his country. So now he said to Perseus: "Be off at once! All your lies about Jupiter and your great deeds will not be of any help to you here." He then seized hold of Perseus and began to thrust him out of his palace. Perseus resisted and at the same time tried to calm Atlas with polite language; but, when this was of no avail, and when he found that the giant was too strong for him (who, indeed, could be as strong as Atlas?) he said: "Then, if you will not give me such a small favor as this, I will give you a different kind of gift." And, turning his own head aside, he held out in front of him the terrible head of Medusa. Immediately Atlas changed into a mountain of the same vast size as he had been in life. His beard and hair became forests; shoulders and arms turned into long ridges; his head was the summit and his bones turned to rock. Then (for such was the will of the gods) he grew in every part to an even more enormous size, and the whole heaven, with all its stars, rested upon his back.

Next day, at dawn, Perseus put on his sandals again, took his curved sword in his hand and cleft his way through the air. After passing over many lands he came in the end to the country of the Ethiopians, over which King Cepheus ruled. As he looked down towards the coasts of this land he saw chained to a rock a most beautiful girl. She stood so still that he would have thought her to be a marble statue, if it had not been for her hair moving in the breeze and her warm tears running down her face. He immediately fell in love with her, and indeed was so struck with her beauty that he almost forgot to move his wings. He alighted close to her and asked her who she was and why she was wearing those cruel chains. At first she made no answer and would have covered her shy face with her hands; but her hands were bound. Her eyes filled with tears and finally, so that he would not think that she had done anything wrong, she told him her story. She was being punished for the foolish words of her mother Cassiope who had boasted that she was more beautiful than the sea goddesses, the Nereids. The result of this boast was that

Neptune, the god of the sea, had sent a great monster out of the ocean to ravage the land. Her father, King Cepheus, had consulted the oracle and had been told that he must sacrifice his daughter Andromeda (for that was the girl's name) to the monster. Now, in chains, she was waiting for the monster to appear. She had been promised in marriage to her uncle Phineus, but he did nothing to help her.

While she was speaking Perseus saw the king and queen, with many people, coming down to the shore, weeping and lamenting for the fate of the innocent girl. Andromeda herself had more reason to weep, for, at the same moment, a great roar came from the sea, and a huge monster appeared with its broad breast making the water surge away at its sides. The girl cried out in terror. Perseus immediately went to her father and mother and addressed them. "My name," he said, "is Perseus. I am the son of Jupiter and of Danaë, whom my father visited in a golden shower. I am also he who killed the Gorgon, Medusa. I think, therefore, that I am quite worthy to be the husband of your daughter. Now, with the help of the gods, I shall attempt to save her and you by fighting with the monster. Will you promise her to me in marriage, if I can save her life?"

Andromeda's parents, not remembering their previous promise to Phineus, agreed at once, and Perseus sprang from the earth and soared into the air. Now the monster, plowing through the water like a great ship was only a sling's shot from the shore. It saw Perseus's shadow on the water and, in its savage rage, began to attack the shadow. But Perseus, like an eagle sweeping from above on a serpent and catching it behind the neck, dived down headlong and buried his sword right up to the hilt in the monster's right shoulder. The wounded beast reared up into the air and plunged down again into the sea which was all purple with its blood. Then it turned and twisted like a wild boar surrounded by a pack of hounds. Perseus on his quick wings avoided its terrible jaws and over and over again darted in to wound it, plunging his curved sword into the great back, which was covered with barnacles, or into its sides or into the place where its fishy tail began. The beast belched blood and water from its mouth as it thrashed about in the sea; the feathers on Perseus's wings grew moist and heavy, but, partly supporting himself on a rock that jutted out from the sea, he thrust his sword three times into the animal's heart. All the shores and the sky resounded with the wild shouts of the people applauding the hero's victory. Cepheus and Cassiope welcomed Perseus as their son-in-law and Andromeda, freed from her chains, was ready to marry him at once.

But before they went to the palace for the wedding feast, Perseus washed the blood from his body and his hands in the waters of the sea. So that the Gorgon's head should not be bruised on the hard rocks, he made a pile of seaweed for the head to rest on. The strange power of the head passed into this seaweed, which became stiff and hard, shriveling up into something like stone. The sea nymphs were delighted with this miracle and brought more and more weeds and twigs, and, when they were hard, carried them back into the sea. This is still the nature of coral, which remains like a twig when it is under the water, but hardens when it is exposed to the air.

Meanwhile Perseus built three altars to the gods who had helped him, and sacrificed on the altars a cow, a young bullock and a bull. Then he claimed his bride, and soon in Cepheus's great golden palace a wedding feast was spread. The walls were hung with garlands; sweet-smelling incense was put on the fires; musicians played on lyres and flutes, or sang to the harp before the Ethiopian nobles who came to witness the wedding.

At the end of the feast, when they had eaten and drunk to their heart's content, the king asked Perseus to tell them the story of his wanderings and of how he cut off the Gorgon's head. Perseus began to tell the tale, but, while he was in the middle of it, suddenly from outside the golden doors came a confused noise of shouting and of the clash of arms, a sound most unfitting to a wedding banquet. The doors were flung open and the king's brother Phineus, holding a long ashen spear, strode into the hall at the head of a great company of armed men. Poising his heavy spear in his hand, he addressed Perseus. "Here I am," he said. "I have come to avenge the theft of my bride. Now your wings will not be able to save you, nor your stories of Jupiter changing into gold."

He was about to hurl the spear, but Cepheus sprang to his feet and cried out: "Brother, what are you doing? It is madness to think of such a crime. If you really deserved my daughter, you should have come and saved her when she was chained to the rock. If it had not been for Perseus, she would now be dead. How then can anyone have a better right to her than he?"

Phineus looked at him grimly and seemed to hesitate

whether to hurl the spear first at his brother or at Perseus. Finally he threw it at Perseus, who lightly avoided it, and it stuck quivering in the bench where he had been sitting. Perseus sprang to his feet, pulled the spear out of the wood, and would have hurled it back at Phineus; but Phineus, the coward, had already taken refuge behind the altar. King Cepheus raised up his hands and cried out to the gods that this act of aggression was against his will and against the laws of hospitality. His brother's men were far more numerous than his own, and there seemed no hope of escape for himself or for Andromeda or Perseus. But, invisible to all, the warrior goddess Minerva was present, protecting Perseus and strengthening his heart.

Now spears were thrown like rain through the hall, past eyes and ears, or cleaving through breastplates or thighs, or stomach. Perseus, with his back against a pillar stood, striking to right and left of him with his curved sword, cutting down men like a mower with a scythe in thick grass. The Ethiopian nobles fought at his side, and behind them were the king and queen with their daughter, crying out to the gods and weeping. Soon the whole floor was drenched with blood and the hall full of the cries of the wounded or the dying. Still more and more of Phineus's army came pouring into the palace, and Perseus, fighting like a tiger, began to feel his strength beginning to fail as he saw no end to his enemies. So he cried out: "Since you force me to do it, there is only one thing I can do. Turn away your heads, all who are friends of mine!" And he raised on high the terrible head of the Gorgon.

As he spoke one of Phineus's strongest captains poised

his spear and shouted out: "Try your magic on someone else! We are not frightened by it."

He was in the act of hurling the spear, and in the very act he turned to a stone statue, with his poised hand stiff and motionless. Others too stopped still and frozen in their places, some with half-open lips, or wide mouths that had been shouting battle cries; others in the act of turning aside from some weapon; others with looks of astonishment on their marble faces. Two hundred had survived the fighting; two hundred statues, in various attitudes, now stood in the halls.

As for Phineus, he had not seen the Gorgon's head, but wherever he looked he saw his friends and comrades turned to stone. Now, with his head turned aside and stretching out his hands, he said: "Perseus, you are the winner. Take away, I beg you, that terrible face that turns men to stone. I admit that I am defeated. I admit that you deserve Andromeda. I ask for nothing, O great hero, except my life."

So he spoke without daring to look in Perseus's direction. Perseus said to him: "You coward, I will not kill you with the sword, but I will make you into a monument which will last for ages and which will please the eyes of my father-in-law and my wife." Then he carried the Gorgon's head to Phineus and, though he struggled to avoid the sight of it, its power fell upon him. The tears on his cowardly face turned to stone: his pleading hands, cringing back and abject look were all fixed in marble.

Now Perseus was victorious over his enemies and safe in the possession of his bride. He had still to discover what had been happening in his absence to his mother in the little island of Seriphus, and he arrived there only just in time to save her life; for, though the good fisherman Dictys had done his best to protect her, King Polydectes had continued to persecute her, and, when Perseus reached the island, she had taken refuge at the altar of Minerva. Perseus went immediately to the palace, where he found the king still as unforgiving and as bitter an enemy as ever. He threatened the hero with violence and even refused to believe that he had killed the Gorgon. "Then believe your own eyes and let them be fixed in the belief," said Perseus, and, holding the head before his face, he turned the king to bloodless stone and in his place made the good Dictys king of the island.

Next Perseus offered to Minerva in her temple the Gorgon's head, and now the goddess carries it fixed in her terrible shield. As for Perseus himself, he went, with his mother and his wife, back to his ancestral country of Argos, feeling sure now that, after his great deeds, his grandfather Acrisius would forgive him, and being anxious too to help him in a war that he was waging. On his way to Argos he stopped at Larissa, where the king of the country was holding athletic sports. Perseus himself competed in the discus throwing event and his first throw went far beyond the boundaries of the stadium and landed among the spectators. Perseus heard with distress that the discus had killed an old man, but his distress was still greater when he learned that the old man was none other than his grandfather Acrisius, who, hearing that Perseus was returning to Argos and still frightened of the oracle, had left his country, little thinking that he would by accident meet his grandson on the way.

After this event Perseus refused the kingdom of Argos. He lived first nearby in the huge castle of Tiryns on the sea, and later founded the kingdom of golden Mycenae. In Athens a temple was built to him and in the temple was an altar specially consecrated to Dictys who had been kind to the hero's mother.

Ceres and Proserpine

THE huge three-cornered island of Sicily is piled upon the body of the rebellious giant Typhoeus, who once dared to attack the gods in heaven. Often he struggles to free himself, but his hands and arms are pinned down by mountains and over his head is the weight of Etna, through which he spouts out ashes and flames in his fierce insatiable rage. But his efforts to push off him and roll away the cities and mountains that cover his body often cause earthquakes, and then Pluto, the king of the underworld, fears lest the earth should split open and light be let in to terrify the thin and trembling ghosts of the dead.

It was in fear of such an event that, on one occasion, Pluto left his shadowy kingdom and, in a chariot drawn by black horses, came to the land of Sicily to inspect its foundations and see that all was well. He examined everything and, finding that there were no signs of weakness anywhere, he laid aside his fears.

But Venus, the goddess of love, who is worshiped in the Sicilian city of Eryx, saw him as he wandered through the land. She put her arms round her winged son, Cupid, and said to him: "My dear son, you who bring me all my power and my success, take your arrows, with which you conquer everything, and shoot one into the heart of that god who rules the world below. The heaven and the sea already own the power of love. Why should the underworld be exempt? Besides it is time that something was done to show our power, because in heaven I am not given the same honor that I used to have. Two goddesses, Minerva and the huntress Diana, will have nothing to do with me, and Ceres's daughter Proserpine, if I allow it, will choose to remain unmarried. So, if you want to increase my power and yours, make Pluto fall in love with Proserpine."

Cupid, at his mother's bidding, took his quiver and chose from his thousand arrows the one that seemed to him sharpest and most sure in flight. He bent the bow across his knee and with the barbed arrow of love he struck Pluto to the heart.

Not far from the city of Etna there is a lake of deep water and here, even more than in the smooth gliding rivers of Asia, one may hear the songs of swans. Woods lie like a crown around the waters and keep off the rays of the sun. In the shade of the branches grow flowers of every color. Here it is perpetual spring, and here Proserpine, with her companions, was playing and gathering violets or white lilies. In her girlish excitement she filled her basket and heaped the flowers in her arms, trying to pick more than any of the others, and suddenly, all in the same moment, Pluto saw her, fell in love with her and carried her off; so violent were the feelings that he had.

Terrified, the girl kept on calling out for her friends and for her mother, especially for her mother. She had, in her struggles, torn her dress at the top and all the flowers began to fall out of it. The loss of her flowers made her cry even more.

Meanwhile Pluto urged on his chariot, calling to his horses by name and shaking the black reins on their strong necks and streaming manes. They galloped through deep lakes, over mountains and past pools steaming with sulphur. Proserpine still cried for help, but only in one case did anyone try to help her. This was the nymph Cyane, who rose waist-high out of the water called after her name, recognized Proserpine and called to Pluto: "You shall go no further! You cannot marry Ceres's daughter against her mother's will, and, as for the daughter, you ought to have wooed her, not seized upon her by force."

As she spoke she stretched out her hands in Pluto's way to prevent him passing, but he, furious with her for obstructing him, urged on his terrible horses and, seizing his royal scepter in his strong arm, struck the pool to its depths. As he struck it, the earth gaped open and down into the earth plunged the black chariot and horses.

Cyane, however, in grief for the fate of the goddess and at the way in which the rights of her own fountain had been set aside, began to melt away in tears and to dissolve into the very waters of which she was the guardian nymph. You might have seen her limbs becoming soft, her bones beginning to bend and her nails losing their brittleness. First the most slender parts melted away; her dark hair, fingers, legs and feet turned into cold water. Then shoulders, back and breast flowed into the stream. Water instead of blood ran through her vanishing veins, and in the end there was nothing left that you could touch.

Meanwhile Proserpine's terrified mother was searching for her, but searching in vain, through every land and every sea. All day she looked for her daughter and at night she lit two torches from the fire of Etna and continued the search in the cold darkness. It would take too long to tell the names of all the lands and seas where she wandered; but, when she had been everywhere in the world, she came back again to Sicily and passed by Cyane. If Cyane had still been a nymph and had not turned into water, she would have told the mother where her daughter was. Now she had no means of speaking, but she did succeed in making some sign, for, floating on her waters, she carried Proserpine's girdle, which had fallen there as she was carried down into the lower world.

When Ceres recognized the girdle, she tore her hair and beat her breast, as if this was the first news she had had of her daughter being stolen away. She still did not know where she was, but she cursed every land in the world and especially Sicily, saying that they were ungrateful to her and did not deserve to have the fruits of the earth. She broke in pieces the plows that turn over the soil; she brought death upon the farmers and upon their animals; she made the harvests fail and put blights and diseases among the young plants. Nothing grew but weeds and thorns and thistles. Throughout the world people were dying of famine or of plagues; and still Ceres was unable to find out where her daughter was.

There is a river called Arethusa, which rises in Greece, then descends into the earth and, after diving below the sea, comes into the light again in Sicily. Now this river Arethusa raised her head from her Sicilian stream, and brushing back her wet hair to the sides of her head, she spoke to Ceres. "O mother of fruit," she said, "and mother of the girl so sought for throughout the world, cease your long labor, and do not be angry with this land which does not deserve your anger, since it did not aid the theft of your daughter. I can give you certain news of her. While I was gliding on my path below the earth, down in the depths of the lower world, I saw Proserpine there with my own eyes. She looked sad certainly, and her face showed that she had not yet recovered from her fear, but she reigns there as the great queen of the dark world, the all-powerful wife of the ruler of the dead."

When Ceres heard these words, she stood still as if she had been turned to stone, and was for long like one out of her mind. Finally grief and pain took the place of horror. She mounted her chariot and went up to the bright shores of heaven. There, with cloudy face and hair all loose, she stood in indignation before Jupiter, and said: "Jupiter, I have come to beg your aid for the child who is yours and mine. If you have no respect for the mother, at least the daughter should touch a father's heart. At last I have found her—if you can call it finding her, when she is still lost to me, and when all I know is where she has been carried away. Let Pluto give her back. Your daughter does not deserve to have a robber for her husband."

Jupiter replied: "It is true that she is our daughter and

I can understand your feelings. Yet, if we call things by their right names, we shall find that no great harm has been done. It was love that caused the theft. Then, if only you will approve the match, Pluto would be no unworthy son-in-law for us. To be the brother of Jupiter and to have in his own realm power as great as mine is a big thing. Nevertheless, if you are resolved on separating them, Proserpine shall return to heaven—but only on one condition, only if she has touched no food with her lips while she has been in the world below. This is the decision of the Fates."

So he spoke, but Ceres was still determined to have her daughter back. This, however, was what the Fates would not allow, because the girl had already tasted food. While she wandered thoughtlessly in Pluto's gardens, she had picked a red pomegranate from a swaying bough, had cut into the yellow rind and eaten seven grains of the fruit. The only one who saw her do this was a boy called Ascalaphus, the child of one of the nymphs of the underground lakes of Avernus. This boy bore witness against her and prevented her return. Then Proserpine in anger dashed water in his face and turned him into a bird, giving him a beak and feathers, big round eyes and long hooked claws. He became that unpleasant and ill-omened bird, the sluggish screech owl.

And now Jupiter in arbitration between his brother Pluto and his sad sister Ceres, divided the year into two parts. Now Proserpine is goddess of both worlds and spends half the year with her mother and half with her husband. Her face became bright again at once, and so did her heart. Before, even Pluto had thought that she looked sad, but now she was like the sun, which, after being hidden behind a rain cloud, comes out again into the open air.

Phaethon

PHAETHON's father was the Sun. Once, when he was talking big and boasting of his father Phoebus, a friend of his could endure it no longer and told him: "You are a fool who believes everything your mother tells you. You are swollen-headed because you imagine Phoebus is your father, when he isn't really your father at all."

Phaethon's face grew red with anger, but a feeling of shame prevented him from doing anything. He went to his mother Clymene and told her how he had been insulted. "What will grieve you all the more, Mother," he said, "is that I, with my fierce noble nature, had to hold my tongue. What a shame it is that such things could be said and yet could not be proved wrong. But you, if I really am sprung from the blood of the gods, give me a sign of my great birth, give me my place in heaven." Then he threw his arms round his mother's neck and begged her for his sake and for the sake of Merops, her husband, and of the future happiness of his sisters, to give him a proof that Phoebus really was their father. As for Clymene, it would be hard to say whether she was moved more by Phaethon's appeal or by the anger she felt at the insult to herself. She raised up her arms to the sky and, looking towards the light of the sun, said: "By that star that flames there with quivering rays, the Sun that hears us now and looks down on us, I swear to you, my child, that he whom you now look at, he, the lord of the world, the Sun, is your father. If what I say is false, then let him withdraw himself from my sight, and let this be the last time that my eyes behold him. But it is not difficult for you to find your father's house. His dwelling place is on the fringes of our land, at the sunrise. If you are brave enough, go there and he will own you to be his."

As soon as his mother had said this, Phaethon leaped gladly to his feet, his mind brimful of heaven. He went through the country of the Ethiopians, whom he regarded as belonging to him, and the Indians who dwell beneath fiery constellations. Resolutely he approached the land from which his father arose.

There stood the palace of the Sun, lofty, with its soaring columns, bright with dazzling gold and metalwork that shone as though it were on fire. Its high roof was overlaid with gleaming ivory and the light of silver radiated from its wide-flung double doors. More wonderful than all this was what art had done; for here Vulcan had made reliefs of the waters girdling the earth, of the whole world and of heaven above. In the water were the sea-blue gods, vocal Triton, and Proteus, who changes his shape, and Aegaeon rising from the waves, pressing down with his elbows the enormous backs of whales. There too were Doris and her daughters. Some seemed to be swimming; others, sitting on a breakwater, were drying their sea-green hair; others were riding on fishes. Their faces were not all alike, nor yet entirely different, but just as sisters should look. On the earth were men and cities, forests and wild beasts, rivers and nymphs and all the other country gods. And above all this was a model of the shining sky. Six signs of the zodiac were on the right-hand door, and six on the left.

Now when Clymene's son had come up the steep path and entered the dwelling of the Sun, he turned his steps straight towards his father's face, but halted while still far off, for he could not bear to approach the light any nearer. Wearing a purple robe, Phoebus was sitting on a throne that shone bright with emeralds. To his left and right were the gods of the Day, the Month, the Year, and the Centuries; and the Hours were there too, standing side by side with the same interval between each of them. Spring was there, with a crown of flowers, and naked Summer, with ears of corn twined into garlands; Autumn too, all stained with the trodden grapes, and icy Winter with bristly white hair. In the center the Sun himself with those eyes that see everything saw the young man standing abashed by the wonder of it all, and said: "Phaethon, my son whom I am glad to own, why have you made this journey? What have you come to seek from this my citadel?"

And Phaethon replied: "O general light of all the world, Phoebus, my father, if you permit me to call you Father and if Clymene is guiltless when she calls you her husband, then, sir, give me some sure sign so that I may be recognized as truly your son, and that I may no longer feel any misgivings over it."

78

He spoke and his father laid aside the fiery rays that shone dazzling round his head. He bade Phaethon approach nearer and he kissed him. "It was a true son of mine," he said, "that Clymene bore, and you yourself deserve to be acknowledged by me. And to remove all your doubt, ask for any gift you like. I will give it to you, and you shall take it. This I swear by the lake below, the lake of Styx that our eyes have never seen, an oath binding among gods."

Hardly had he finished speaking when Phaethon demanded his father's chariot, and that he might be allowed for one day to drive his winged horses.

Phoebus repented of his oath. Thrice and four times he smote his gleaming forehead. "Rash, indeed," he said, "were the words I spoke and which you have seized upon. I wish that we were not allowed to make promises. Child, I admit to you that this was the one thing I should deny you. I may still try to dissuade you. What you desire is dangerous. You are asking for something big, Phaethon, something which is too much for the strength you have and for your tender years. Your fate is that of a mortal; yet you are begging for power that belongs to gods. Indeed you go further and are ignorantly aiming at something which is beyond the reach of the gods themselves. Much as others might like it, there is none but I who can ride that fiery car. Even the ruler of huge Olympus, he who rains thunderbolts from his right hand, even he will not guide this chariot. And what is mightier than Jove?

"The first part of the road is steep and the horses, though they are fresh in the early dawn, can hardly make the ascent. The middle of the course is in the topmost height of heaven. I myself might well fear, my heart might well flutter in my breast as I look down from that height on sea and land. The last part of the way is downhill, and demands a sure hand on the reins. There the goddess of the sea, Tethys herself, into whose outspread waves I sink, often fears lest I may be hurled into them headlong. Remember, too, that the sky itself turns in a continual revolution, whirling the constellations with it round and round in its rapid course. I struggle against it and this force, which governs all else, does not govern me; my swift track cuts across. Now suppose I gave you the chariot. What would you do? Could you steer a course against the rolling poles to prevent the motion of the sky from carrying you off your proper way? Perhaps you imagine that in those parts there are sacred groves, cities of the gods, shrines rich in gifts. Actually the road is beset with traps and runs between the shapes of beasts. Even if you keep in the right path and are not led astray, you will have to go straight between the horns of the Bull, past the Archer's bow and the Lion's savage jaws, past the Scorpion on the one side and the Crab on the other, each stretching wide the cruel pincers of his claws. And it is no easy matter to control those horses, spirited as they are with the flames that burn in their hearts and which they breathe from their mouths and nostrils. Even I can only just make them obey me when their fierce spirits have grown hot, and they toss back the reins from their necks. Child, let me not give you a gift that will bring ruin upon you. Be sensible, now that you have a chance, and ask me for something else. Is it a sure sign that you want? I give you a sure sign by this fear that I feel for you, and I prove myself to be your father by showing a father's solicitude for his son. I wish that you could look into my heart and see there all the anxiety that your father feels. Now look round on all the riches that the world contains, and from all the good things of earth and sky and sea ask something for yourself. It will not be refused to you. It is only this one thing that I am unwilling to give, and it is a thing that is more likely to hurt than to honor you. You are asking me to hurt you, Phaethon, not to help you. Poor innocent, why do you put your arms round my neck to coax me? Have no fear; whatever you desire will be granted (have I not sworn by the waters of Styx?). But, I beg you, be more sensible about what you want."

He had said what he could to restrain the boy, but Phaethon refused to listen, and, burning with desire for the chariot, pressed on with his demands. So his father, when he had delayed as long as he might, led the young man to the lofty chariot, the work of Vulcan. The axle was made of gold, and the pole was made of gold; the rims of the wheels were golden, and the spokes radiated out in silver. Chrysolites and jewels shone in rows along the yoke, and shimmered with the light they got from Phoebus.

With swelling heart Phaethon stood staring at it all and examining the workmanship. Then, while he was so occupied, suddenly in the glowing dawn Aurora woke, and threw wide the purple doors opening on to her halls that are full of roses. The stars scattered and Lucifer, who keeps his station longest, followed in the rear of their retreating ranks. When he saw Lucifer on his way to the earth, and the world beginning to blush red, and the tips of the moon's horns as it were fading away, then the Titan ordered the swift Hours to yoke his horses to the chariot. Quickly the goddesses did as they were told. They brought out from their lofty stables the fire-breathing horses, fed on juices of ambrosia, and they laid over their necks the jingling reins. Then Phoebus put some magic ointment on his son's face, so that he could endure the rushing flame, and on his head he placed the crown of rays. He sighed, for he felt a foretaste of the sorrow that was coming, and it was with great anxiety that he spoke: "My dear boy, try to listen at least to what I am going to say now. Keep a firm hand on the reins, and don't use the whip. The horses go fast enough of their own accord. The difficulty is to hold them in. And don't go straight through all the five zones of heaven. The track curves across, running only through three of them, avoiding both the south pole and the bitter winds of the north. This is your way, and you will see clearly the marks of my wheels in the sky. Then, so that both heaven and earth may have the right amount of heat, you must neither drive too low down, nor make the chariot climb to the top of the sky. If you go too high you will set the houses of the gods on fire, if too low, you will burn up the earth. The safest way is between the two. Don't go too far to the right, in the direction of the writhing Snake, or too far to the left in the direction of the constellation Altar, but keep straight between them. The rest I must leave to Fortune, and I pray that she will look after you better than you have looked after yourself. But, while I have been speaking, damp night has reached her boundary on the western sky line. We can wait no longer. My presence is required; darkness is scattered and the dawn is shining. Grasp the reins in your hand, or, if only you will change your mind, take my advice and not my chariot. While there is still time, and you are still standing on solid ground, not yet swept away by the chariot you have so foolishly begged for, allow *me* to give light to the earth, so that you can watch me and be safe."

Phaethon swung his young limbs into the airy chariot, took his stance and felt a thrill of joy as he fingered the light reins. Then he thanked his father for the favor that he had granted so unwillingly. Meanwhile the four winged horses of the Sun, Fire, Dawn, Brilliant and Flamer were filling the air with their whinnying, fiery breath, and pawing impatiently against their barriers. Tethys, who knew nothing of her grandson's fate, swung back the gates, and gave them the freedom of the immeasurable sky, and they plunged out into the road and, cleaving the air with their feet, split through the clouds before them, passing by on their soaring wings the winds of the east that rose with them. But the weight of the chariot was light, too light for the horses of the sun to feel. The yoke did not have its usual weight on their backs; and, like curved ships that are underloaded roll and go unsteadily through the sea because of insufficient ballast, so the chariot without its usual freight swung about in the air, tossing up and down as though it were empty. The four horses, as soon as they realized this, got out of hand, left the well-worn track and set off in a different course. Phaethon grew frightened. He did not know how to handle the reins which he held, nor where the proper road was, nor, even if he did know, could he steer the horses into it. Then the cold stars of the north felt for the first time the heat of the sun's rays and tried in vain to plunge into the forbidden sea. But when poor Phaethon looked down from the height of heaven on the lands lying far, far beneath him, he grew pale and suddenly his knees began to tremble in panic. Through all that light a mist rose before his eyes. Now he would give anything never to have touched his father's horses. He wished that he had never known whose son he was, and never had his prayer answered. He is willing enough now to be called the son of Clymene's mortal husband, now that he is carried along like a ship in a hurricane, when the helmsman has dropped the rudder and can do nothing but pray. What is he to do? Much of the sky is behind him, but much more is in front. He measures both distances with his eyes, looking now towards the region of the sunset, which he is fated never to reach, now towards the region of the dawn. Not knowing what to do, he stands there stupefied, without letting go of the reins, yet without the strength to hold them properly. He does not even know the horses' names. He sees too, scattered over the colored heaven, strange wonders, and stares in terror at the shapes of huge beasts. There is one place where the Scorpion stretches out the pincers of his two claws; with crooked arms and tail his shape extends over two of the zodiac's signs. When the boy saw him covered with black poisonous sweat he thought he was going to sting him with his menacing curled tail. He grew cold with fear, lost all control, and dropped the reins.

As soon as the horses felt them lying loose along their backs, they rushed off headlong. With no one to hold them in, they went through the unknown regions of the air, and wherever their fury carried them, there they rushed unchecked. In the height of heaven they run among the fixed stars, tearing the chariot along through trackless ways, now climbing high into the air, now hurtling headlong again towards the earth. The Moon saw with amazement her brother's horses running below her own. The clouds caught on fire and smoked. The mountaintops broke into flame, and the earth, with all the moisture dried out of it, split into great cracks. The grass turned white in the heat; trees with all their leaves burned up, and the crops took fire all the more easily because they were ripe. Worse still, great walled cities were destroyed. The flames burned whole nations to cinders. The forests and the mountains were on fire. Athos was blazing and Cilician Taurus and Tmolus, and Oeta, and Ida with its many fountains dry at last. Helicon, where the maiden muses go, and Haemus was ablaze; the fires of Etna roared into the sky with twice their usual strength. The two peaks of Parnassus, Eryx, Cynthius and Othrys were blazing; now at last Rhodope must lose her snow; Mimas, Dyndyma, Mycale and religious Cithaeron all burn. Arctic weather does not protect the Scythians. Caucasus blazes with Ossa and Pindus and Olympus, greater than both, the airy Alps and cloud-rolling Apennines.

Wherever he looked Phaethon saw the world on fire. He could no longer support the heat. The air he breathed was like a blast from the depths of a furnace. He felt the chariot grow white-hot beneath his feet; he could not hold his head up against the cinders and flying sparks; hot smoke rolled all round him, and this pitchy shroud prevented him from knowing where he was or whither he was going, dragged along at the sweet will of the flying horses. It was at this time, they say, that the Ethiopians got their black skins, because all the blood was drawn to the surface of their bodies by the heat. Then too Libya was drained of moisture and this was the origin of the Sahara desert. The nymphs let their hair flow loose and wept for their fountains and their pools. Rivers are lucky enough to have banks wide apart, yet this did not preserve them. Steam rose from the middle of the Don's stream. Babylonian Euphrates is aflame and Orontes and rushing Thermodon; Ganges, Phasis and Danube; Alpheus boils; the banks of Sperchius are blazing; the gold that the river Tagus carries in its sand is liquefied by the flames. The swans that live in the Cayster, and used to sing in throngs along the banks, are scorched in midstream. The Nile fled in terror to the end of the world, and even now no one has discovered where it hid its source. Its seven mouths lay empty and filled with dust, seven channels and no water in any of them. The same thing happened to the rivers of Thrace, the Hebrus and the Strymon and to the streams of the west, the Rhine, the Rhone and the Po and that river which was to have the mastery of the world, the Tiber.

The whole earth split into fissures and through the cracks light pierced down into Hades to frighten the king and queen of the dead. The sea shriveled up so that what had once been an ocean became a plain of dry sand; and now the islands had their number enlarged by the appearance of mountains which previously had lain deep down beneath the water. Fish went for the bottom and the arched dolphins no longer dared to leap up into the air as they used to do. Dead bodies of seals, belly up, floated on the surface. The story goes that Nereus himself and Doris with her daughters, hiding in the caves of the deep sea, could not even then keep cool. And Neptune, looking furious, three times raised his arms out of the ocean, and each time was unable to stand the fiery atmosphere.

But Mother Earth, who was surrounded by sea, between the waters of ocean and her own streams, which had shrunk and run for hiding into the dark recesses of her body, raised her stifled face, scorched though she was. As she drew her hand across her forehead the earth quaked and settled down lower than it was before. Then the holy mother spoke: "King of Heaven, if this is what you will and what I have deserved, then why is your lightning idle? If I must die by fire, then let it be by the fire *you* throw. Death would be more bearable if I knew that it was from you that it came. As it is I can scarcely open my mouth to say what I am saying" (for the smoke was choking her). "See how my hair is singed and how the sparks are pouring into my eyes and over my lips! Is it for this that I am fertile and hardworking, that I bear the furrowing of curved plows and the scraping of hoes, and am hacked about all the year round; that I provide good nourishing fodder for cattle, corn for the race of men, and frankincense for you? Even supposing that *I* deserve to be destroyed, what harm has the sea done, or your brother Neptune? Why are the waters that he won by lot shrinking away and sinking ever lower from the sky? And if you can not feel for me or for your brother, then at least have pity on heaven, which belongs to you. Look around you. Smoke is pouring from each of the two poles. If once the fire eats well into them, your own palace will collapse. Look at Atlas and see what trouble he is in. He can only just carry on his shoulders the white-hot firmament. If sea and earth and the kingdom of heaven perish, we shall fall back again into original chaos. O snatch away what is still left from the flames, and save the universe!"

So the earth spoke, and then, since she could bear the heat no longer and could say no more, she sank into herself and into the caverns nearest to the ghosts below.

Then the Almighty Father called all the gods to witness, and particularly him who had given Phaethon the chariot, that, unless he acted, the whole world would perish miserably. He climbed up high to the top of heaven, to the place where he goes when he spreads clouds over the world, or stirs up the thunder, or shakes out lightning through the air. But then he had no clouds to spread and no rain to let fall from heaven. He thundered, and balanced a thunderbolt in his hand; then, letting it fly from beside his right ear, he shot it at Phaethon and hurled him out of the chariot and out of life as well, quenching with his own raging fire the fire that Phaethon had kindled. The horses panicked and sprang apart from each other, tearing their necks from beneath the yoke and leaving the reins snapped in mid-air. The harness, the axle with the pole torn from it, spokes of the broken wheels, and various fragments of the shattered chariot he scattered far and wide.

As for Phaethon, flame raged through his red hair. Over and over he fell headlong in his long descent from heaven, like a shooting star, which, though it never actually reaches the earth, looks as though it is going to do so. He fell into the river Eridanus far from his native land, in a completely different quarter of the globe, and the river water washed over his smoking face. The Nymphs of Hesperia took the body still smoking from the forked flame, and buried it. On the tombstone they wrote this verse:

> Phaethon rode the sun, and here's his tomb.
> His daring was the reason for his doom.

The Great Flood

THERE was such wickedness once on earth that Justice fled to the sky, and the king of the gods determined to make an end of the race of men. Then Jupiter let loose the South Wind, and the South Wind came with drenching wings. He veiled his terrible face in pitchy darkness; his beard was heavy with the storm and his hair was streaked grey with rain. Clouds sat upon his forehead; water poured from his feathers and the folds of his garments. He squeezed in his fist the hanging masses of cloud, and there was a crash. Thick vapors fell from the air, and Iris, the messenger of Juno, dressed in rainbow colors, carried water to feed the clouds.

The crops were battered to the ground and farmers wept for their fallen hopes; for all the year's work had turned out to have been useless.

Jupiter's anger was not confined to his province of the sky. Neptune, his sea-blue brother, sent the waves to help him. He summoned the rivers and when they had entered the palace of their lord, he said: "No need for many words. Just pour out the whole of your strength. That is what I want. Open all your doors, let nothing stop you, but give free rein to your flowing streams!" So he commanded, and they went away. Then the springs ran unchecked and the rivers rolled unbridled to the seas. Neptune smote the earth with his trident and the earth shivered and shook, giving free passage to the waters under the earth. The rivers broke their bounds and went rushing over the lowlands, dragging along with them fields of corn and orchards, men and beasts together, houses and religious buildings with all their holy images. If there was any house left which could stand up against the flood without crashing down, yet its roof was under water and its turrets were hid by the waves eddying above. Soon there was no telling land from sea. The whole world was sea, except that this sea had no shores.

You could see the men, one getting up on to a hill, another sitting in his curved boat, using oars now in the very place where he had been plowing only a moment before. Another man is sailing over corn fields or over the roof of some great submerged house; yet another is catching fish among the topmost boughs of an elm. Perhaps their anchors grapple the green grass of meadows, or the curved keels scrape over vines growing under water. And where the light-limbed goats used to crop the turf, now ugly-looking seals go flopping about.

Under the water the sea-nymph Nereids are staring in amazement at woods, houses and cities. The forests are now full of dolphins who dash about in the tops of the trees and beat their tails against the swaying trunks. You might see a wolf swimming with a flock of sheep, yellow lions carried away by the water, and tigers too. The wild

boar, though he is strong as a thunderbolt, cannot help
himself, nor is the stag's fleet foot any use to him. He too
is swept away; and the birds, after they have wandered
far and looked everywhere for a place to alight, fall into
the sea too weak to move their wings.

The sea, in its boundless power, had flattened out the
smaller hills, and waves, never seen there before, were lap-
ping round the crests of mountains. Nearly all the men
perished by water; and those who escaped the water, having no food, died of hunger.

There is a place called Phocis, a rich land, while there
was any land, but at that time it was part of the sea, just
a huge plain of hurrying water. There is a mountain there
whose twin peaks seem to aim at the stars. It is called Parnassus and its summit is above the clouds. All the country
round was under water, but Deucalion with his wife, in a
little boat, got to this mountain and landed. There was no
man more good or more devoted to fair dealing than Deucalion, and there was no more reverent woman than his
wife, Pyrrha.

Now when Jupiter saw that the whole earth had become
one lake of running water, and that from so many thou-
sands of men and women only this one man and this one
woman were left, and that both of them were innocent,
both good decent folk, then he dispersed the clouds, made
the north wind roll away the rain, and unveiled again the
whole vault of heaven. The sea no longer raged. The ruler
of the deep laid aside his three-pronged spear and calmed
the waters. He called for sea-blue Triton and soon Triton's
head rose out of the deep, and his shoulders, all overgrown
with barnacles. Neptune told him to blow on his horn of

shell the signal for retreat to waves and rivers. He took up his bugle, a spiral shell, twisted at the mouthpiece and opening out wide at the other end. When he draws in his breath and blows into this bugle the sound goes out from the middle of the sea to the ends of the world. So now as soon as the shell had touched the lips and dripping beard of the god and the blast had been blown calling the retreat, the sound was heard by all the waters of earth and sea, and they obeyed, one and all. Now the sea has shores again, streams run brimming their channels, rivers go back to their beds, and the hills begin to appear. The earth emerges; land grows as water shrinks away, and as time passes woods appear below the naked summits of the hills, though mud still sticks to the leaves of the trees.

So the world came back again. But when Deucalion saw it all empty, and all the countries lying desolate in a tremendous silence, tears came into his eyes and he spoke thus to Pyrrha: "My sister, my wife, you, the only woman left, once it was our family, our birth and our wedding that brought us together, but now our dangers are another bond. We two are all the inhabitants of all the lands that the sun looks on when it rises and when it sets. The sea has the rest. And even now we cannot be sure that we are safe. The terror of those clouds still sticks in my mind. Poor creature, what would you feel like now, if you had been preserved from fate without me? How would you endure terror, if you were alone? Who then would be trying to console you? As for me I am sure that if you had been drowned I should go after you and be drowned too. Oh how I wish that I had the skill of Prometheus, my father, and could get all the people back again and pour life into

94

molded clay! As it is the whole race of mankind is comprised in us two, and we seem to have been preserved just as specimens of humanity. Such was the will of heaven."

So he spoke, weeping, and then they decided to pray to the powers above, and ask for help from the holy oracle. Together they went straight away to the waters of Cepheus, which were not yet running clear, but they knew where the shallows were and so passed through them. They took water from the stream and sprinkled it on their heads and garments; then they went to the shrine of the holy goddess and saw the roof of the shrine shining with foul sea-slime, and the altars with no fire burning on them. When they reached the steps of the temple, they both fell on their faces and reverently kissed the ice-cold stones. Then they spoke: "If the powers of heaven can feel anything or be at all moved by the prayers of the just, if the anger of the gods is not inflexible, then tell us, O Themis, what skill there is by which we can repair the ruin of the race. Lend thine aid, O most merciful one, to the drowned!"

Moved with compassion, the goddess gave her answer: "Go forth from the temple. Veil your heads and unloose the girdles of your garments. Then scatter behind you on the ground the bones of your venerable mother."

For a long time they stood still in amazement, till Pyrrha first broke the silence, and said that she could not do what the goddess had bidden them. Her lips trembled as she begged for pardon; but how could she dare to wound her mother's ghost by throwing her bones about? All the time they pondered within themselves and revolved in their minds the difficult words of the goddess's reply, so dark to understand.

Finally Deucalion found soothing words to calm his wife. "Oracles," he said, "are good things and could never tell us to do anything bad. Now, either my usual intelligence has gone astray, or else 'our venerable mother' is the earth. And by 'bones' I think the oracle must mean the stones that are in the body of the earth. It is stones that we are told to scatter behind us."

Pyrrha was certainly impressed by her husband's interpretation, but still they hardly dared to hope. So mistrustful were they both of the commands of heaven. Still there was no harm in trying, so they went out of the temple, veiled their heads, girded up their tunics, and, as they had been told, scattered stones behind them as they went. Antiquity is our evidence for what happened next. Otherwise I doubt whether anyone would believe it. For the stones began to lose their hardness. Little by little they grew soft, and as they softened they began to take a new shape. They went on growing; something less hard than stone was stirring within them, something like humanity, although it was not quite clear yet, but more like pieces of sculpture that have only just been begun, which are more or less like what they are meant to be, but are not yet quite rounded off. All the earth and mud which stuck to the stones became flesh; the solid core became bones; veins in the mineral were still veins, but now they had blood in them. And in a short time, by the power of the gods, all the stones which Deucalion had sown grew up into men, and women sprang from the stones which Pyrrha scattered.

So we human beings are a hard stubborn race, well used to labor; and that is how we prove that this story of our birth is true.

Jason

JASON, who won the Golden Fleece, was the first man to build a ship. He was also the first to lead an expedition of Greeks against the East. His father, Aeson, had been driven from the throne of Iolcos by Pelias, his half-brother, and had been forced to live in a poor house, with all his wealth and all his honors taken away from him. At this time Jason was a small boy, not strong enough to defend himself, and Aeson feared for his son's safety. He therefore put the boy in the care of the wise centaur, Chiron, half man and half horse, who lived in the wooded mountains around Iolcos. In music, medicine and archery Chiron was the most famous of teachers, and in all these subjects Jason quickly became himself an expert.

As he grew to manhood his beauty, his intelligence and his strength were alike remarkable, and Chiron, proud of his pupil, advised him to consult the oracle as to what he should do with his life. "Return to Iolcos," the oracle replied to his question, "and demand from Pelias the kingdom that rightfully belongs to your father."

Jason therefore said good-bye to Chiron and came down

from the mountains to the plain. He carried spear and sword, and was dressed in a leopard skin. On his way to Iolcos he had to cross a river which at this time of year was swollen with rain water from the melting snow on the mountain peaks. When Jason reached this river he saw waiting on the bank an old woman who asked him to help her across. This he readily agreed to do, but, when he was in midstream, he was surprised to find that, in spite of his strength, the old woman seemed to weigh him down, as though she were heavier than the size of her would suggest. As he struggled through the river, one of his sandals slipped from his foot and was swept away by the stream.

When he reached the other side, he set the old woman down and turned to look at her, but, as he turned his head, she had disappeared, and he knew that he had been visited by one of the gods. It was in fact Juno, the wife of Jupiter, who had been neglected by King Pelias, and who, ever afterwards, helped Jason and supported him.

After addressing a prayer to the goddess, Jason went on his way to the city, and here his yellow hair, his strong and beautiful appearance, soon attracted attention. Among those who looked with interest at the stranger was King Pelias himself, but he looked at Jason not only with admiration but also with fear. This was because an oracle had told him that one day he would have his kingdom taken from him by a man wearing only one sandal. He immediately summoned Jason to him and asked who he was and what was his business in Iolcos. Jason boldly and in front of all the people gave his name and said that he had come to claim the kingdom that had been wrongfully taken from his father. As he spoke the people admired the young man's courage and showed plainly that they were on his side. All that Pelias could do was to attempt to gain time. He therefore said to Jason: "If you are indeed worthy of what you claim, you must prove your worth. You are young, and you should have some noble deed to your credit before you can be acknowledged fit to rule. What I wish you to do is this—to avenge the death of our relative Phrixus and to bring back to Greece the Golden Fleece."

Jason knew the story of Phrixus, since he had been told this and other stories of gods and heroes by the centaur Chiron. He also knew that Phrixus had been related to him, since his own grandfather had been the brother of Athamas, who in the end had been driven mad by Juno, but who had had by his first wife, Nephele, two children who were called Phrixus and Helle. Later Athamas had married Cadmus's daughter Ino, and Ino, jealous of her step-children, had plotted to kill them. But the boy and girl were saved by a ram with a golden fleece, which was given to them by Mercury. On this animal's back they escaped from Thebes and even crossed the sea. The girl Helle grew tired on the way and fell into the sea which is still called the Hellespont after her; but Phrixus arrived safely at the court of King Æetes who ruled over the land of Colchis at the far extremity of the Black Sea. Little at this time was known of Æetes except that his father was the Sun and that he was a wizard with strange powers. Instead of treating Phrixus hospitably, Æetes had murdered him in order to have the golden fleece of the ram which Phrixus had sacrificed when he arrived in Colchis.

Many people would have shrunk from what appeared to be so desperate a task as the recovery of the Golden Fleece, but Jason, though he knew that King Pelias hoped and expected that this adventure would cost him his life, determined nevertheless to undertake it. He let it be known throughout Greece that he intended to lead an expedition to the east, and from all over Greece young men and heroes came to Iolcos, eager for the glory of sharing in the ambitious enterprise. In the end fifty-three men and one woman sailed on the *Argo*, a miraculous ship built by the craftsman Argos. It had in its prow a beam cut in the oak woods of Dodona. This beam was capable of speaking in a human voice and pronouncing oracles.

The ship was launched to the music of the famous singer, Orpheus, who went himself on the expedition. Tiphys was the steersman. Other heroes who sailed with Jason were Hercules, the son of Jupiter, Lynceus, whose eyesight was so keen that he could easily see quite small objects at a distance of nine miles, Aesculapius, the great doctor, Calais and Zetes, the winged sons of the North Wind, Meleager of Calydon and many others. The one woman who sailed was Atalanta, famous as a huntress and as a runner. All these heroes are known as the Argonauts, since they were sailors in the *Argo*.

The Voyage of the Argonauts

Very many adventures took place on their way through the sea to Colchis. First they landed at the island of Lemnos and were surprised to find not a single man in the place. It was governed entirely by women under their queen, Hypsipile.

The reason for this unusual state of affairs was the anger of Venus. The women of the island had neglected to sacrifice to the goddess of love, and Venus determined to be revenged on them. So she brought it about that they were all afflicted with a most unpleasant smell, which made them not only unattractive, but positively disgusting to their husbands. The result was that their husbands took other wives, either from among their slaves or from among the women of the mainland opposite. In great anger at having been treated in this way the women of Lemnos met together and contrived a cruel plot—that each of them should, in one night, murder her male relations, so that there should be no more men left on the island. This terrible plot was actually carried out, except that the queen Hypsipile spared the life of her father Thoas.

It was not long after this murder of the men that the Argonauts landed in Lemnos, and found that the women, now restored to their usual condition, were very glad to see them. In particular Queen Hypsipile fell deeply in love with Jason, and Jason promised her that, after he had won the Golden Fleece he would return to Lemnos and make her his wife. As we shall see, he did not keep his promise and, in the end, Hypsipile was forced to leave the island, was captured by pirates and sold as a slave. But so hospitably were the Argonauts received at Lemnos that they stayed there for a whole year. Others besides Jason made promises of fidelity to the women who had entertained them, but none of these promises were kept.

After a year's stay at Lemnos, the *Argo* put to sea again
and at Cios, where they had landed to find a fresh supply
of water, Jason lost the services of one of the strongest
and bravest of his companions. Hercules was devoted to
his young page Hylas, a beautiful boy who, with the
others, took his jar for carrying water and went into the
woods to find some fountain or pool. Wandering further
than the rest he came in the silence of the midday to a
beautiful pool of clear water, with poplars growing near it.
Over the pool hung dewy apples that no one had culti-
vated, growing on trees that few if any eyes had seen before. All around on the cool turf grew white lilies and red
poppies. It was a place sacred to the nymphs called
Dryads, and Hylas, loving the beauty of the scene, enchanted with the flowers and the bright water, forgot his
task and busied himself with picking the flowers. In the
end he lay down beside the lake and, propping himself on
his right elbow, leaned down to the water to drink. The
nymphs of the lake saw him as he leaned towards them
and wondered at his beauty. Raising their heads and their
wet arms above the surface, they gently drew him below
the lake to be their playfellow. Hylas, as he felt himself being drawn under, cried out for help, and his friend Hercules, though at some distance away, heard him. Then
for a whole day Hercules and the rest searched the woods
and the glades which resounded to the cries of "Hylas!
Hylas!" No trace, however, could be found of the missing
boy. There was a long journey to go and the Argonauts determined to leave; but Hercules refused to go with them.
As they set out again into the sea he remained behind and

for long he sought in vain for his friend. The boy was never found; but to this day, in memory of his loss, the people of this country go every year through the woods calling out "Hylas! Hylas!" as though there was a hope of discovering him.

Among the Argonauts were the two brothers Castor and Pollux, sons of Zeus. Pollux was particularly skillful as a boxer, and this skill was of great service to his companions when, after leaving Hercules behind, they came to the kingdom of King Amycus, the son of Neptune, whose custom it was to challenge all strangers to a boxing match. Those who lost the match (and so powerful was the king that he had never been defeated) were compelled to serve him as slaves or else were put to death. The Argonauts, having chosen Pollux as their champion, watched anxiously as the two boxers fastened to their hands the great gloves of leather with iron bars along the padded knuckles. With such gloves it was not impossible for a man to be killed. They and the followers of King Amycus stood in a circle to watch the fight, and soon it was evident that, though perhaps Amycus was the stronger of the two, Pollux had the greater skill. He lightly avoided the king's enormous blows and, leaping inside his guard, raised great red marks on his ribs and stomach as he struck with the heavy gloves. He maneuvered carefully, so that the king would have the sun in his eyes, and now, changing his tactics, he began to strike at the face and soon his opponent was spitting out blood and teeth mixed together. Finally, growing desperate, Amycus seized hold of Pollux's right arm with his left and, while he was so held, smashed a blow at him which, if it had landed, would certainly have killed him. But Pollux slipped his head aside and, striking out from the shoulder, struck Amycus such a blow on the temple that the bones cracked and the king fell to the ground in a heap. Pollux might well have killed his enemy, but instead he made him swear a great oath never again to molest strangers with his bullying ways.

Next the Argonauts came to the court of the blind King Phineus, who was gifted with prophetic powers. The king indeed attempted to entertain them hospitably, but, no sooner were they seated at the tables and the food was set out than there swooped down from the air three terrible monsters called the Harpies or "Snatchers." These creatures had women's faces and the bodies and wings of large vultures. They pounced upon the tables, flapping their huge wings, fouling everything with the mess they made, knocking over the goblets of wine and filling their greedy and disgusting mouths with whatever they could take up. So Phineus, in the midst of all his riches, had not been able for years to eat one meal undisturbed. This was a punishment which had been sent him by the gods, because he had used his prophetic power to reveal secret things. Now, however, the day of his deliverance had come, for among the Argonauts were the two winged sons of the North Wind, Calais and Zetes, who were, indeed, his brothers-in-law, since Phineus had married their sister Cleopatra, who had not lived to see her husband blind and persecuted.

Now the young children of the North Wind drew their swords and sprang into the air, since they were winged. The Harpies fled away, turning and twisting to avoid the thrusts of the brothers' pursuing swords, and the chase went on over land and sea till, high in the sky above a group of islands that lay like jewels in the blue water, Iris, the goddess of the rainbow, appeared and said: "Cease your pursuit, Calais and Zetes! It is not for you to destroy the Harpies. But Jupiter promises that never more will they come to afflict Phineus. Now return, and ask the king to tell you of the dangers that lie in front of you and Jason and your friends."

The brothers obeyed her and, lightly turning in the air, flew back to the palace of Phineus where, for the first time in years, the king was able to enjoy an unmolested meal.

When the meal was over, Jason turned to the king and said: "We have been glad to help you to escape from your persecution. Now we ask you to help us. Tell us, if you will be so kind, what other dangers we are to expect before we reach the land of Colchis."

Phineus turned his blind eyes in Jason's direction. "Your greatest dangers," he said, "will be in the land of Colchis itself, and of these I may not speak. What I can tell you is that, before you enter the Black Sea, at its very gateway, you will have to pass between two blue rocks that are called the Symplegades, or Clashers. Those rocks guard the straits. At one moment they move apart from each other; at the next they dash together with such violence that anything, whether it be a bird or a ship, that is caught between them is immediately crushed and broken to pieces. When you reach these rocks, what I advise you to do is to take a pigeon and let it go free. If the pigeon succeeds in flying unscathed between the rocks, that will be a sign to you that the gods are not unfriendly. Watch the rocks carefully, and, when they move apart, row with all your might. If you pass through safely, you will have done a glorious thing, for you will have made a road for ever from Greece into the eastern sea."

Jason and the Argonauts listened to him with astonishment, and not without fear. This was a danger which they had never imagined. Nevertheless they had not come so far only to turn back again, and, after sacrificing to the gods, and having enjoyed for some days the hospitality of Phineus, they again set to sea. The winds favored them, and it was not long before, on the distant horizon, they saw what appeared to be sheets of water spouting into the air. As they drew nearer they were aware of a noise like thunder, and soon they could see clearly the two blue and craggy rocks that intermittently leaped apart and sprang clashing together, sending up clouds of water as they met, and deafening the ears with the roar of their impact. Beyond them was the surface of another sea, and there was no way to reach it except between these clashing mountains.

Jason took his stand in the stern so that from there he could urge on the rowers. First, he prayed to all the gods and especially to Juno, and liberated a white dove. All watched the dove closely as it sped straight as an arrow between the rocks. It flew fast, but, as the rocks closed roaring together, it looked as though the dove had been caught and crushed between them. The next moment, as the spray subsided, the Argonauts raised a shout of joy. One of the dove's tail feathers indeed was swaying up and down on the water, but the dove itself, as they could see, had flown through in safety and was already winging its way over an unknown sea.

Jason called to his companions and urged them (not that there was any need of urging) to use every ounce of their strength when he gave the word. Again the rocks clashed together. Then, as they parted, Jason shouted out the word of command. The rowers bent over their oars and the ship's timbers seemed to shiver as she leaped through the rough and foaming water. The steersman, Tiphys, held her on a straight course, and she seemed to move as though some divine power had given her wings. With a tremendous splintering crash the two rocks came together again; but the *Argo* was through. A piece of the rudder had been smashed to pieces, but the ship and all aboard her were safe and sound. The Argonauts looked at one another with wide and startled eyes, hardly believing that they had escaped so great a danger. Friend embraced friend and offered up prayers of thanksgiving to the gods. Then they looked back in astonishment at the sudden silence that had fallen on the sea. The two rocks, which never before had made way for any man or any ship, now stood motionless, one on each side of the channel. So they stand to this day, giving an easy passage to sailors from the west. The Argonauts, keeping the northern coast of Asia Minor upon their right, sailed on to Colchis at the limit of the sea.

The Golden Fleece

In the end they reached the swift and muddy waters of the river Phasis. This is the land from which pheasants came in the first place. Rowing up the river they reached the court of King Æetes, and there, surrounded by his brave companions, Jason explained the reason of their coming and asked that the Golden Fleece should be returned to the kinsmen of Phrixus.

The king, seeing so many and such brave champions in front of him, was, for the moment, at a loss for a reply. Finally he spoke: "I admit that your claim is just, but I can grant it only on these conditions. Tomorrow at sunrise, you must yoke my bulls to the plow. You must plow a field and then sow there the teeth of a dragon. If you are successful in these tests, you may take the Golden Fleece, but you must take it yourself and singlehanded from the serpent who is its guardian. These are my terms. Tell me if you will accept them."

The gods made Jason bold. "They have helped me so far," he thought. "Will they not help me to the end?" He looked resolutely at the king. "I accept your conditions," he said. "But if I do my part you must do yours."

The king smiled as he agreed. Only he and his daughter Medea, who was sitting at his side, knew that the tasks he had proposed were beyond the strength of any mortal man. As for Medea, her mind was carried this way and that way as she looked now at her father, to whom she owed her loyalty, and now at the brave and beautiful stranger whom she was seeing for the first time. "What I feel," she said to herself, "is either love or something like what people call love. I cannot bear the thought of this stranger perishing and I want to save him. Yet, if I do so, I shall be betraying my father and my native land. I know that I should support my father; yet, though I see clearly what I ought to do, my feelings lead me in exactly the opposite direction. Would it not be cruel to allow this young man to feel the fiery breath of my father's bulls, to fight with an army springing from the earth, or to be given as a helpless prey to the terrible dragon? Yet these things must happen to him if I do not help him. But then, when he has the Golden Fleece, what will become of me? I cannot bear to lose him. If I can help him, he must take me with him to Greece and make me his wife. I should have to leave my father and my home, but I should be the wife of a great hero and I should be renowned myself for my magic arts and for saving all the best of the Greeks."

So she thought to herself, and in the evening, when she was on her way to sacrifice to Hecate, the great goddess of witches and enchantresses, she met Jason in a wood and fixed her eyes on his face as though she were seeing him for the first time. Jason took hold of her right hand, and, in a low voice, begged her to help him, promising that, if she did so, he would take her away with him and marry her. She burst into tears and said: "I know that what I am doing is wrong, but I shall do it. Only swear that you will keep your promise."

Jason then swore by Hecate, by the all-seeing Sun and by all the gods that he would be true. Medea gave him the magic herbs and told him how he must use them in the perils of the next day.

When dawn came crowds flocked to the sacred field of Mars and stood all round it on the heights above. King Æetes, in a purple robe and carrying an ivory scepter, sat on his throne with Medea at his side and his people all round him. Suddenly into the field came the bulls. They had hooves and horns of brass, and through their iron-hard nostrils they blew out fire and smoke. The grass shriveled and caught on fire as they breathed on it, and the noise of their breathing was like the noise of a roaring furnace. Jason went to meet them, and, as he approached, they turned their terrible faces upon him, pawed the ground with their brazen hooves and shook their metal horns, filling the whole air with fiery bellowings. The Argonauts, as they watched, stood stiff and silent in terror; but Jason went up to the bulls, and, so great was the power of the magic herbs that he had received, did not feel the burning of their fiery breath. With one hand he boldly stroked their swinging dewlaps; then he put the yoke on their necks and forced them to draw the heavy plow and furrow up the field that had never felt iron before. The men of Colchis gazed at him in astonishment. The Argonauts raised a great shout and added to his courage by their applause.

Next Jason took the dragon's teeth from a brazen helmet and began to sow them in the plowed field. The teeth, steeped as they were in powerful magic, grew soft in the earth and began to swell up into new forms. Just as a child grows gradually inside the mother's body, and does not come out into the world until it is a fully shaped human creature, so these seeds grew under ground and did not emerge to the surface of the earth till they had taken on the shapes of fully-grown men, complete with weapons which they clashed together. When the Greeks saw this army of warriors preparing to hurl their sharp spears at Jason's head, again their faces fell and again their hearts failed them. Medea herself was frightened and grew pale as she saw one man surrounded by so many enemies. Silently, as she sat there, in case the charms she had already given him should not prove strong enough, she began under her breath to mutter other magic spells. But Jason took up a great rock and hurled it into the middle of the earth-born army. This had the effect of turning all their rage and anger upon themselves. Man fought man until the whole lot of armed men had perished by each other's hands.

Then the Argonauts thronged round Jason, embracing him and cheering and congratulating him on his victory. Medea, too, would have liked to embrace him, but was afraid of what people might say. All she could do was to look at him with silent joy and thank the gods who had given her such powerful spells.

All that remained now was to face the terrible dragon that guarded the Golden Fleece. It was a creature with a great crest on its head, a three-forked tongue and curving hooked teeth. It was coiled around the stem of the tree where, through the thick dark leaves, glowed a gleam of gold, showing where the fleece was. Jason sprinkled on the dragon some juices from herbs of forgetfulness which Medea had given him. Then three times he recited a spell strong enough to make stormy seas calm or to force swollen overflowing rivers back into their beds. Gradually and for the first time sleep came over the dragon's eyes. Jason threw the heavy fleece across his shoulder and, fear-ing some treacherous attack from King Æetes, hurried to his ship with the Greeks and with Medea, who had saved him. Quickly they went aboard and quickly sat down at the rowing benches. They were sailing down the river almost before Æetes had realized what had happened.

When, however, the king discovered that his daughter had fled with Jason, he determined to overtake them and sailed in pursuit with his whole fleet. Once more Medea saved her husband and the Greeks, but she only saved them by doing a terrible deed. She had taken with her her little brother Absyrtus. Now she killed the boy and threw on the water pieces of his body, so that King Æetes would delay his pursuit in order to collect the fragments of his son's body for burial. Thus the Argonauts reached the open sea in safety. In their peril no one of them had blamed Medea for her cruel act, but afterwards many were to reproach her for it. Now, their task achieved, they sailed joyfully back to Iolcos.

Jason and Medea

One might have expected that now Jason, who had performed the most noble exploit, and his beautiful wife Medea, the greatest of enchantresses, would have been happy; but, whether because of the cruel murder of Absyrtus or for some other reason, events were to turn out far otherwise.

When first the Argonauts returned in triumph to Iolcos the city was full of glad crowds and everything that could be done was done to celebrate the safe and glorious return of the heroes. Incense was heaped on the flames of the altars. Great feasts were held, and bulls with gilded horns were sacrificed to the gods. But one man was unable to take part in all the rejoicing. This was Jason's father, Aeson, who was now so old and so close to death that he could not leave his house. In pity and distress Jason spoke to Medea. "My dear wife, to whom I owe my safety, you have given me everything already; but, since your spells are so strong, can you not perhaps give me one thing more? Can you not take away some of the years that I myself am fated to live, and give these to my father, so that he may live longer?"

Medea remembered how she had deserted her own father, and she was touched by Jason's love for the old Aeson. "Certainly, Jason," she said, "I would not, even if I could, take away any years from your life. But, if Hecate will help me, I will try to do something better still. I will try to make your father young again."

In three nights' time it would be full moon. When the third night came, and all the earth lay white beneath the moon's round and complete splendor, Medea put on a loose flowing dress and went out of doors. She was barefooted and her hair was loose on her shoulders. Men, beasts and birds were sunk in deep sleep; there was no movement in the hedgerows; the leaves hung motionless on the trees; the dewy air was still and silent. Only the stars twinkled, and, stretching her arms towards the stars, Medea turned round in a circle three times (since the gods of witchcraft are pleased with uneven numbers), three times sprinkled fresh water on her head, and three times pronounced a howling cry. Then she kneeled down on the hard ground and prayed: "O Night, you who hide our mysteries, and Hecate, you who are the goddess of witches and enchanters, and Earth, you who provide us with our magic herbs, now I need your help. Already by my spells I have made rivers run backwards, drawn the moon down from the sky, uprooted forests and mountains, and compelled the ghosts to rise from their tombs. Now I have need of drugs which will turn old age back again to youth, and now I know that I shall find them, for the stars flash out their reply to me and I see my chariot, drawn by winged dragons, coming to me through the air."

As she spoke her magic chariot came to her out of the night. She mounted it and, after she had stroked the drag-ons' necks, she flew away to the plains of Thessaly and for nine days and nine nights plucked from river beds and forests and open ground the herbs and grasses she needed. Some she pulled up by the roots and others she cut with a bronze sickle. Finally, after wandering far and wide, she returned in her chariot. The dragons that drew it had only smelled the magic herbs, but even so their old gnarled skins changed into new skins of the most brilliant colors.

When Medea reached her home, she would not yet go indoors or allow her husband or anyone else to touch her. She built two altars out of turf, one to Hecate and one to Youth. By each altar she dug a ditch and filled the ditches with the blood of a black sheep which she sacrificed. On the top of the blood she poured bowls of wine and of warm milk.

Then she ordered her servants to bring old Aeson out

of the house. They carried him on a stretcher, since he was too weak to move and indeed on the point of death. Medea, by her spells, put him into a deep sleep and laid him on a bed of herbs. Then she told Jason and all the rest to retire. None must be allowed to witness her secret rites.

They retired and she, with her loose hair streaming behind her, went from altar to altar, kindling the flames and dipping the wood that she burned in the pools of blood. Then in a bronze cauldron she began to mix her magic brew. Into the cauldron went the roots that she had cut in the valleys of Thessaly, together with seeds and flowers and pressed juices. To these she added some pebbles from the far east and some sand from the stream of Ocean. Then she put in some frost which had been collected under the full moon, also the wings with some of the flesh of the hideous screech owl, and the entrails of a werewolf—the animal that can change from a wolf into a man. There, too, in the cauldron was the scaly skin of a water snake, the liver of a stag, the eggs and head of a crow that had lived for nine generations. All these and a thousand other strange things were mixed together in the pot, and, as the pot began to simmer, Medea stirred it with an old dry branch of olive. This old dry stick, as it touched the hot liquid, first of all began to grow green, then put out leaves, and then was covered with fresh-grown olives. And whenever drops of the mixture bubbled over on to the ground, the earth where the drops fell became green and flowers began to grow there.

As soon as Medea saw this, she drew her sword from its

sheath and cut the old man's throat. She let out all the old blood and instead of it filled his body, partly through the lips and partly through the wound, with her magic potion. As the new blood spread in his veins, Aeson's grey hair and beard began to turn black; his thin scraggy limbs put on flesh; his pale neglected cheeks flushed red; the wrinkles disappeared, and he rose to his feet in all the strength of youth. As he looked in amazement at himself, he remembered that this was what he had been like forty years before.

Unfortunately, however, Medea was not content with this act of mercy. She determined to use the fame which she had won to revenge herself cruelly on Pelias, who had taken Aeson's kingdom from him and who had refused to surrender it to Jason. In order that she might carry out her plan she pretended that she and Jason had quarreled and she went to the house of Pelias, where she was kindly received by his daughters. These girls were naturally interested in all Medea's magic powers, and Medea was constantly telling them of how she had made old Aeson young again. The daughters of Pelias asked her whether she could not do the same thing to their own father. Medea craftily pretended to hesitate, so that in the end they would be all the more willing to do as she told them. After appearing to ponder things over in her own mind she said: "It is necessary for you to have confidence in me, and so that you may really feel confidence, I ask you to bring me the oldest ram in all your flocks. You will see that my charms will make him into a lamb again."

At once the daughters of Pelias brought a woolly ram

so ancient that he could scarcely stand, with great horns curving round his hollow temples. Medea cut his old throat, hardly staining her sword, since the blood was so thin, and then plunged the body into a bronze cauldron where powerful herbs were boiling in the water. These herbs made the body shrink and made both the horns and the years of the animal disappear. A thin bleating noise came from inside the cauldron and, while they were still wondering at this noise, out skipped a lamb which, after stumbling a little on its unsteady legs, ran frisking away to look for some udder to give it milk.

After having seen this, the daughters of Pelias were all the more eager that Medea should try her arts on their father. This was exactly what Medea wanted for the success of her treacherous plan.

Night came and she put over a fire a cauldron of boiling water. Into the water she put herbs which had no magic powers at all. Then she led Pelias's daughters into the bedroom where their old father was asleep. "Why do you hang back now?" she said to them. "Draw your swords and let out the old man's blood, so that I may fill him with new blood. If you love your father, do as I tell you."

They indeed shrunk from such a deed, but in the end, feeling that their father's future happiness depended on them, they plunged their swords into his body. The old man, mortally wounded, woke from his sleep and began to cry out, "My daughters, what are you doing to me?" Then Medea cut his throat with her sword and plunged the body into the boiling water which immediately extinguished any life that was left.

So terrible a revenge pleased neither Jason nor the people of Iolcos. In spite of Jason's great fame, both he and Medea were forced to flee from the country. They went to Corinth, the city between two seas, where, after the voyage of the Argonauts, Jason had brought the *Argo* ashore and dedicated it to the gods. Here for ten years they lived happily, and two children were born to them. This happiness, however, did not last.

Whether because of Medea's savage nature or because he wished to gain advantage by being related to the King of Corinth, Jason decided to leave his wife. He forgot the promises which he had made to her when she saved his life at Colchis, and he asked Creon, the king of Corinth, for the hand of his daughter Glauce. Creon was glad that his daughter should marry the famous leader of the Argonauts, but he was frightened of Medea. He therefore decided to banish her and her children from Corinth.

After he had told her that she must go, Medea, with great difficulty, persuaded the king to allow her to stay for one day in order to make her preparations. What she prepared was a terrible revenge. She pretended that she was not angry either with Jason or the princess Glauce, and she sent her children to the palace with a beautifully woven robe and a golden diadem as a wedding present. The young princess hurried to try on the fine clothes. She put the diadem on her head and dressed herself in the beautiful dress. But both dress and diadem had been steeped in terrible poisons. As the princess walked about her room, now and again stretching out a foot to see how the folds of the robe hung, she suddenly gave a cry of pain.

The dress was clinging to her flesh and burning it. Her head was all on fire and, as she shook her head to get rid of the diadem, the fire blazed out all the more fiercely. No one dared touch her until her old father Creon, hearing her cries, came to her and embraced her as she lay dying. Then the fire settled on him too. For all his efforts he could not tear himself away from his daughter's body which clung to him like ivy round a tree. Both of them lay dead, killed by Medea's enchantments.

Meanwhile Medea had done a deed even more dreadful than this. Determined to make Jason suffer in every way, she killed her two children and, when Jason, in rage and misery at the murder of his bride, came to her palace, she appeared before him in her winged chariot with the bodies of the children in her own keeping. She would not even allow him to touch the bodies or give them burial, but flew away to the land of Athens, where the old king Aegeus sheltered her.

As for Jason, in spite of the great fame of his youth, his later years, deprived of his kingdom, his wife and his children, were miserable. One day in his old age he was sitting beside the sea in the shadow of his old ship, the *Argo*, which had been drawn up on land to be a monument. But now many of the timbers had rotted away, and, as Jason sat there, a great beam from the prow broke and crashed on his head. So Jason was killed by the very ship which had made him famous.

Echo and Narcissus

THE famous Theban prophet Tiresias gave many true answers to those who sought his advice. Among these answers was one that he gave to a nymph, the mother of a beautiful boy called Narcissus. She had asked the prophet whether her son would live to old age, and the prophet replied: "Only if he never knows himself." For a long time there seemed to be no meaning in the reply, but in the end the death and the strange falling in love of Narcissus showed that the old prophet was right.

For when the boy had reached his sixteenth year he was loved by very many young men and very many girls. But in his beautiful body there was so much hard pride that he would have nothing to do with any of them.

Once in the forest when he was driving the frightened deer into his nets, a nymph called Echo saw him. Echo was neither able to begin a conversation nor to keep quiet when others were talking. At this time she had a body and was not, as she is now, just a voice; yet her speech was just as it is now. She could only repeat the last words that others spoke. Juno had made her like this, being angry with her for engaging her in long conversations in order that she would not inquire too closely into what her husband Jupiter was doing.

Now, when she saw Narcissus wandering in the pathless forest she immediately fell in love with him, and, hiding herself, she followed in his footsteps. How much she longed to speak to him and say soft things in his ear! But this she could not do. She had not the power to speak first and could only wait for him to speak so that she could use his own words.

It happened that Narcissus had become separated from his companions and he called out: "Is there anyone here?" Echo answered him, "Here!" and he looked all round him in amazement. "Come to me then!" he shouted out and at once came Echo's reply: "Come to me then." Again he looked round and, as no one appeared, he called out: "Why are you avoiding me?" Again the same words came back to him. He stood stock still, wondering what this answering voice could be, then cried out: "Let us meet here!" "Meet here," Echo replied and never gave a reply which delighted her so much. And, following up her own words, she came out of the woods where she had been hiding, went up to Narcissus and wished to throw her arms round his neck. But he fled from her and, as he fled, he cried out: "Take your hands off, and don't touch me. May I die before I let you have your way with me!"

"I let you have your way with me," she answered, and then she could speak no more. Spurned, she lay hid in the woods, covering her blushing face with leaves, and ever afterwards lived in lonely caves. Her love however remained and indeed, through pain at what she had suffered, grew even stronger. In sleeplessness and worry her body wasted away. She became thin and wrinkled: all the moisture in her body vanished into the air: only her bones and her voice were left. Her voice still remains. Her bones, they say, were turned to stone. Still she hides in the woods and is seen no more in the mountains. But everyone can hear her, since her voice, and only her voice, is still alive.

Not only Echo, but many nymphs of the water and of the mountains, were despised by Narcissus. So too were the companies of young men. In the end one of those who had been treated so proudly prayed to the gods: "May he fall in love like this himself, and not gain the thing that he loves!" It was a just prayer and the goddess Nemesis heard it.

There was a bright pool with shining silvery water, a place where no shepherd had ever come or goats that feed on the mountains or any other cattle. No bird or beast or even a bough falling from a tree had ever ruffled its mirrored surface. There was grassy turf round the margin, cool and soft from the water, and there were thickets interlaced that kept away the heat of the sun. Here, tired out with hunting, Narcissus came and, pleased with the place and with the spring of water, he lay down beside the pool to quench his thirst. But as he did so, he was filled with a different kind of thirst. Seeing himself in the water he looked with amazement at himself and stayed there motionless, with the same expression on his face, like a statue, staring into his own eyes, at his smooth cheeks, his neck like ivory, the white and red of his beautiful face. Without knowing that what he saw was himself, he fell in love with what he saw, and as he looked with love at his own reflection, the face into which he gazed looked back at him with love too. Often he vainly plunged his arms into the water, trying to clasp the neck that he saw there. Never did it dawn upon his foolish mind that the image which he pursued would turn away if he turned away himself, that what he longed for was only a shadow.

Neither hunger nor desire for sleep could tear him away from the place. Stretched out on the shady grass he continued to gaze with eyes that could never be satisfied at that deceitful image of himself. His own beautiful eyes brought him to death. He raised himself a little from the ground and stretched out his arms to the surrounding trees. "O you woods and forests," he said, "you who have witnessed so many loves, has anyone been more unfortunate in love than I? I see, but I cannot touch what I desire. And it is not as though there was a great ocean between us, or long roads or mountains or city walls. We are only separated by a little water. And the face I look at looks back at me with love, smiling when I smile, weeping when I weep. Why then does it always escape me?"

So he spoke and, half out of his senses, looked back again at the image in the water. As his tears fell on the surface, the reflection seemed to shiver and break, and over and over again he cried out: "O do not leave me!" So, lying there, he began to pine and waste away, like yellow wax in the heat or like frost in the rays of the morning sun.

Echo, though she was angry with him, and remembered how he had treated her, was sad when she saw him. When he cried out: "Alas!" she repeated the word after him. His last words, as he stared into the water were: "Farewell, face that I have loved in vain!" and Echo replied to him: "I have loved in vain." Then he let his tired head drop on the green grass. Death closed the eyes that had wondered at their own beauty. Even when he was received into the lower world of the dead, they say he kept gazing at his face reflected in the dark pool of Styx.

The nymphs of the forests and of the rivers mourned for him and Echo answered their cries. They were making ready his funeral with torches and a pile of wood for burning. But the body was nowhere to be found. In its place they found a flower. It has a yellow center with white petals surrounding it.

Meleager of Calydon

MELEAGER was the son of the King of Calydon. The three Fates, Clotho, Lachesis and Atropos, were present at his birth. Clotho foretold that he would be a great hero; Lachesis said that he would be gifted with enormous strength; Atropos declared that his life would last as long as the piece of wood now burning on the fire.

His mother, Althea, when she heard this, immediately took the log from the fire, plunged it in water and kept it carefully, knowing that on it depended the length of her son's life.

As Meleager grew up, all that the Fates foretold came true. He was one of the heroes who sailed with Jason in the *Argo*. His courage and skill saved his country and his father from many enemies. But he is chiefly remembered for the hunting of the Calydonian boar, a noble exploit, though one which was to prove disastrous to him.

Meleager's father, at a great Harvest Festival, had sacrificed grain to Ceres, wine to Bacchus, and olive oil to Minerva. To all the other gods also he sacrificed as was proper. But he neglected the goddess Diana and left her altars without incense or offerings. The gods feel anger as men do. "I may be unhonored," Diana said, "but I shall not be unavenged," and she sent into the fields of Calydon to avenge herself an enormous wild boar, as big as the bulls one finds in northern Greece and bigger than the bulls of Sicily. His eyes flashed with blood and fire; his neck was like a solid ridge; the bristles along his back stood stiff like the shafts of spears; hot foam flecked his shoulders as he roared and grunted; his tusks were as long as those of the Indian elephant; lightning came from his mouth; the grass shriveled up when he breathed on it.

He trampled down the young corn as it began to show; he ravaged good crops that farmers were ready to harvest. Threshing floors and granaries were empty. Heavy bunches of grapes with their long green tendrils were thrown down and trodden under foot; so were the branches and trunks of the ever-leafy olive. Then he turned his rage on the farm animals. Shepherds and sheepdogs could not protect their flocks, nor could fierce bulls preserve their own herds. The country folk fled in all directions and did not consider themselves safe unless they were behind city walls.

Meleager now summoned together from all over Greece a band of young men who were eager for the glory of killing this boar. Many of the heroes who had sailed with Jason in the *Argo* came now to Calydon. Among them was Jason himself, Castor and Pollux, and many others. There was Peleus, the father of Achilles, Nestor, a young man who in his old age was to fight in the Trojan War, Laertes, the father of Ulysses, Theseus with his great friend Pirithous. There also came Atalanta, the famous huntress of the Arcadian woods. A brightly polished brooch secured her dress at the shoulder; her hair was done simply, tied in a knot behind her head; from her left shoulder swung an ivory quiver which rattled as she moved; in her left hand she carried her bow. Her face was of the kind that might be called boyish in a girl and girlish in a boy. As soon as he saw her, Meleager fell in love with her. "Happy indeed," he said, "would be the man that this woman should think worthy of her!" His own modesty and the importance of the occasion prevented him from saying more. The time had come for the great conflict with the boar.

There was a forest where the trunks of trees stood close together, untouched for ages by the axe. It started from the plain and, rising up the hills, looked down on the fields that sloped away from it. On reaching this forest, some of the hunters began to set out the nets, others loosed their hounds, others followed tracks worn on the ground, all eager to meet danger. So they came to a deep valley into which flowed the streams of rain water from the higher ground. In the bottom of the valley grew willows, sedge, marsh grass, bulrushes and various kinds of reeds. Out of all this undergrowth they roused the boar, which charged down upon its enemies like lightning struck out from the shaken clouds. The trees and bushes were laid flat as he rushed forward; there was a crash of falling boughs as he swept through the forest.

The young men raised a shout, gripped their spears firmly, and held them poised, with the broad iron heads pointing ready to throw. The boar charged on, with deadly

sideways movements of the head scattering the barking
dogs that tried to hold him. The first spear thrown missed
its mark and grazed away some of the bark of a maple
tree. The next one, thrown by Jason of Iolcos, seemed certain to stick in the animal's back, but it had been thrown
with too much force and went too far. In this first volley
only one spear hit the boar and from this spear, as it flew,
Diana tore the point, so that only the wooden shaft
reached its mark. Even this blow roused the animal's
anger. It rushed on like a thunderbolt. Its eyes glared and
it seemed to breathe out flame from its mouth. As a rock
hurled from a catapult comes whirling through the air at
walls or towers with soldiers on them, so this bloodthirsty
wild boar charged down relentlessly on the young men. It
knocked over two of them at the right of the line, but their
comrades picked them up and carried them to safety. Another hunter, Enaesimus by name, was not so lucky. As he
turned to run away he fell down with the muscles behind
his knee ripped through by the boar's tusks. Nestor of
Pylos would never have lived to go to the Trojan War if
he had not used his spear as a jumping pole and leaped
up into the branches of a nearby tree. Safe in the tree, he
could look down on the enemy he had escaped. The boar
sharpened his tusks on the bark of an oak and then, still
furiously raging, made a great gash in the thigh of another
hunter. Then the twin brothers Castor and Pollux ran forward, both easily to be recognized on their snow-white
horses, both poising their spears together and hurling them
hrough the air. Indeed they would at least have drawn
olood with their weapons, if the bristly creature had not

plunged into the thick woods out of reach of weapons or
of horses. The heroes followed after, and now Atalanta
fitted a swift arrow to the string and shot it from her
curved bow. The arrow sped over the top of the boar's
back and stuck behind his ear. Blood began to ooze over
the bristles. Meleager was just as pleased with her success
as she was herself. He was the first to see the blood and
the first to point it out to the rest. "You shall have the prize
that your courage deserves," he cried to her.

The men meanwhile blushed with shame at being out-
done by a woman. They urged each other on by shouts,
gaining courage themselves from the noise they made, and
hurling their spears in no proper order, so that their throwing missed its effect. There was one of them called Ancaeus
who was armed with a double-headed axe. He ran in front
of the others and spoke boastfully to them. "Now look, my
friends," he said, "and I shall show you how much better
a man's weapons are than a girl's. Leave it all to me. Let
Diana herself, with her bow and arrow, try to protect this
boar, whether she likes it or not he will fall by my hand."

So, puffed up with pride, he spoke, and, digging his toes
into the ground, he stretched up with his axe held above
his head, ready to bring it crashing down upon his enemy.
But the boar rushed straight at him, aiming his tusks at
the lower part of the stomach where wounds bring death
quickest. Ancaeus fell with his stomach ripped open.
Streams of blood soaked the ground.

Then Theseus threw his heavy spear with its bronze
point. It was well aimed, but on its way caught against the
leafy branch of an oak and missed its mark. Jason again

hurled a javelin, but had the bad luck to miss the boar and strike an innocent dog, which the spear pinned to the ground.

Meleager himself had a different fortune. He threw two spears, the first of which stuck quivering in the earth. The second one however fixed firmly in the middle of the boar's back. Then he sprang forward and, while the enraged animal turned round in circles, spouting out blood and foam, he pressed on his attack and finally plunged his shining spear right into the beast's shoulder. His friends shouted aloud to show their joy and hurried up to press him by the hand. Then they gazed in wonder at the enormous body lying stretched out over so much ground. Even now it seemed scarcely safe to touch it, but they all dipped their weapons in its blood.

Meleager stood with his foot on the boar's terrible head, and said to Atalanta: "You were the first to wound the boar, and you must have the prize that you deserve. I should wish my glory to be shared with you." He then gave her the trophies of the chase, the skin with its stiff bristles, and the head with its huge tusks.

She was delighted with the gift, and delighted too with the giver, but the others were jealous and resentful. Angry murmurs were heard on all sides.

Two of the hunters, Plexippus and Toxeus, were uncles of Meleager, being brothers of his mother Althea. These two, shouting and waving their arms, cried out: "Put the prize down, girl, and don't think that you can escape with what belongs to men! Don't think either that your beauty is any advantage. Meleager may be in love with you, but will not be able to help you." So they deprived her of her gift and him of the right to give it.

This was too much for Meleager. He bit his lips in rage and cried out: "You that take what belongs to others, I will show you the difference between boasting threats and real action." Immediately he turned on Plexippus who was expecting no such thing, and plunged his sword into his heart. Then, while Toxeus hesitated what to do, his thoughts balanced between the wish to avenge his brother and the fear of sharing in his fate, Meleager cut his hesitation short and thrust the sword still warm from the blood of one brother into the body of the other.

Meanwhile Meleager's mother Althea was bearing gifts to the temples of the gods in honor of her son's victory. But as she was on her way she saw the two dead bodies of her brothers being carried into the city for burial. Then she beat her breast and filled all the place with her cries. Instead of her golden robes she put on black. When, however, she heard that the murderer was her own son, her grief fell away. She now turned from weeping to the desire for vengeance.

In a secret part of the house there had been kept for a long time the log of wood which had been on the fire at the moment of Meleager's birth and which, by being kept safe, had kept Meleager safe himself. Now Althea brought this log out from its hiding place, and told her servants to put pine branches and small kindling wood together and light the unkind fire. Four times she started to throw the log on the fire; four times she stopped herself in the moment of doing so. Her feelings as a mother and her feelings as a sister were on different sides and pulled her in different directions. Sometimes her face looked like the face of one in anger, sometimes like the face of one who feels pity. And when fierce burning of anger seemed to have ended her tears, then the tears would come again. So, like a ship driven one way by the wind and another way by the tide feels both forces and moves now this way now that, Althea was swayed in opposite directions, laid aside her anger and again took it up.

Finally her love for her brothers overpowered her feeling for her son. As the fire grew hot, she took the log and said: "These hot flames must now devour my own flesh. I hate the deed that I do, yet how else can I satisfy my brothers' ghosts who are crying to me for vengeance? My son deserves to die, yet why should I be the one to bring him his death? And by killing him I shall be killing myself. Yet in front of my eyes are my dear brothers' wounds. I do what I must do."

So she spoke. Then turning away her face, and with her hand trembling, she threw the fatal log into the middle of the fire. It groaned or seemed to groan as the flames fastened on it and the unwilling fire burned it up.

Meleager far away in the forest and ignorant of what was happening felt himself burning in the same flame. He felt fire raging through his body and in strong endurance he tried to force down the pain. Still he was sad that his death was coming to him not in battle but in this unmanly way, and he called Ancaeus happy for dying as he did. On the point of death, he cried out, groaning with pain, for his old father, his brothers and loving sisters, and his wife. No doubt he cried out for his mother too. As the fire increased so did his pain. They both died down together, and as Meleager's spirit vanished into the thin air, so the white ashes settled on the hearth.

Now high Calydon was brought low. Old and young, rich and poor joined in the lament, beating their breasts and tearing their hair. Meleager's father lay stretched on the ground, complaining that he had lived too long. Now he had lost his wife too, for Althea, in horror at her deed, had punished herself by thrusting a sword through her own heart. No one could describe the grief of Meleager's sisters. Crying and wailing, they kissed over and over again their brother's body, and, when the body was consumed by the funeral fire, they gathered up the ashes and pressed them to their breasts. For long they wasted away in mourning at his tomb, till Diana, who was satisfied with her vengeance, took pity on them, put long wings upon their arms, gave them beaks instead of mouths, changed them into speckled guinea fowl and sent them into the air.

The Story of Theseus

His Journey to Athens

NOT far across the sea from Athens lies the city of Troizen. To this city once came Aegeus, King of Athens, and there he and Aethra, daughter of the King of Troizen, had a child who was called Theseus.

Aegeus returned to Athens but, before leaving, he took his sword with its ivory sheath and put it under a great rock. Then he said to Aethra: "When the boy is strong enough to lift this rock, let him take his father's sword and come to me in Athens."

By the time that Theseus was sixteen, he was not only strong but intelligent and ambitious. When his mother showed him the rock, he easily lifted it up and took from beneath it the sword, still bright and shining in its close-fitting ivory scabbard. His next task was to visit his father in Athens. Instead of going there by sea, which was the safe and easy way, he decided to travel by land. This meant a journey through narrow mountain passes and rough ways, through a country infested with robbers and wild beasts. Not for a long time had anyone from Troizen dared to go this way.

The first part of the road lay along the seashore, and Theseus had not gone far before he met a giant called Periphetes or "Famous," who was the son of Vulcan, the god of fire, and carried a huge iron club with which he would beat out the brains of all travelers who attempted to pass him. Like his father Vulcan, he limped in one foot, but he was immensely strong and quite without mercy. Theseus was well trained in the use of the sword, and, being nimble on his feet, avoided the great swinging blows of the giant's club, thrusting his sword over and over again into his enemy's body. So he slew him and went on his way along the solitary road, carrying with him as a trophy the great club.

The road to Athens went north to the Isthmus of Corinth, where two seas are separated by a narrow strip of land. Near here lived the brigand Sinis, called "the Pine-bender," because, when he seized upon a traveler, he would bend down two pine trees and, after tying their tops to the arms or legs of his miserable victims, would let the trees go, thus tearing limb from limb the men or women who had fallen into his power. This notable robber attempted to overpower Theseus so that he could treat him in the same way as he had treated so many others. But Theseus smote him to the ground half stunned with his club and, bending down two pine trees himself, fastened them to Sinis's own limbs. Then he released the trees, and the criminal met the same death that he had so often inflicted on innocent people. Henceforward the road to the Isthmus from the south was open to all travelers.

Theseus now turned eastward. Ahead of him on his right was the island of Salamis and on his left the two rounded citadels of Megara. Near here, on cliffs that towered above the sea, lived Sciron, another brigand of the most evil fame. First he would plunder travelers and then force them to wash his feet in a bronze bowl. While they were doing this, he would suddenly, from where he sat, kick them over the cliff into the sea. There their bodies were devoured by a large tortoise who for many years had swum around the base of the cliffs, fed continually on human flesh.

Theseus had heard of this cruel murderer, and when he met him in the narrow pathway over the rocks, he pretended to be willing to wash his feet. But, just as Sciron was preparing, with one blow of his foot, to hurl him into the sea, Theseus gripped his foot firmly, swung him round and, grasping him by the shoulder, threw him into the sea himself. Far below he saw the sea turn white as the body fell, and then he saw the back and head of the monstrous tortoise coming to the surface for his last meal of men's flesh.

There was yet another wicked enemy to strangers whom Theseus treated in the same way as he had treated others. This was the strong man Procrustes who wrestled with all travelers and, when he had overcome them, would make them lie down on his bed. If their bodies were too short for the bed, he would rack their arms and legs with weights or hammer them out until they were long enough to fit. If they were too tall to lie on it, he would chop pieces off their limbs until they fitted exactly. At last this cruel robber had met his match. Theseus, after wrestling for long with him, threw him to the ground. Then he bound him to his own bed and, though here his body was exactly the right length, he cut off his head.

Theseus was now close to Athens and had conquered all the human enemies whom he would meet on his way. What he met with next was a monstrous sow, which for long had terrorized the villagers in the country districts near Athens itself. Some say that this sow had been the mother of the great boar that Meleager killed in Calydon. At all events she was an immense animal, strong and savage, and used to root up the crops with her snout, drag down the vines from their supports and kill and eat young children and defenseless old people. Theseus went out alone to hunt this sow. He avoided the animal's furious charges and each time she swept past him he planted a hunting spear in her back. Finally, with a blow of the club he had taken from Periphetes he killed the sow and enabled the country people to continue unmolested their work in the fields.

Soon afterwards from the top of a hill he saw below him the city of Athens which poets have called "violet crowned," because, as the sun sets, the ring of rocky hills that surround the city turns from shade to shade of violet and amethyst. He drew nearer and came to the great stone walls of the citadel, or Acropolis, where his father's palace stood. Having accomplished such brave deeds on his journey, he was confident that his father Aegeus would receive him kindly.

As it happened, however, he very nearly met his death at his father's hands. The enchantress Medea had fled to Athens after her cruel murder of her own children and of the royal house of Corinth. In Athens Aegeus had protected her, had made use of her magic powers and by her had had a child. Medea, by her enchantments, knew that Theseus was now on his way to Athens. She was jealous of the fame that he had won already and she wished her own son to have the throne of Athens after Aegeus's death. She therefore pretended that she had discovered by her magic arts that the stranger who would shortly arrive in Athens was a criminal who had come to murder the king. She instructed Aegeus to give him, as soon as he arrived and without getting into conversation with him, a cup of wine into which she had put deadly poisons. Aegeus believed her, and, when Theseus arrived and stood before him, he himself handed to his son the poisoned cup. Theseus raised it to his lips and was about to drink when, at the last moment, Aegeus noticed at Theseus's side the ivory scabbard of the sword he had left long ago under the rock in Troizen. He dashed the cup from the young man's lips and folded him in his arms. Then he turned in anger upon Medea who had so nearly made him the murderer of his own son. But Medea, knowing that this time no excuses could save her, had mounted into her winged chariot and disappeared through the air. This was the last of her wicked deeds. Some say that she returned to her country of Colchis and became reconciled with her family, but nothing really certain is known about this.

Even now Theseus and his father were not entirely secure in the land of Athens. First there was the hero Pallas who, with his fifty sons, tried to seize the kingdom from Aegeus. They made a treacherous attack on Theseus, but he, fighting back at them with a small company of friends, killed every one of them.

Then, at the time when Theseus reached Athens, the whole plain to the north, the plain of Marathon, where later the great army of the Persians was destroyed, was ravaged by a great bull. The people of the district had turned in vain to their king for help. No man or body of men dared encounter this fierce tremendous animal. Theseus went out to Marathon alone. He captured the bull alive, bound it with ropes and brought it back to Athens. There, after a triumphant procession through the streets, he sacrificed it to Minerva, the goddess of the city. The joyful throngs of people acclaimed him gladly as their future king and as a hero who had driven from their country and its surroundings both robbers and wild beasts. No one in the world, they said, except Hercules, had done such deeds.

Theseus and the Minotaur

Athens was now safe and peaceful within the borders of her own land, but still every year she had to make a cruel sacrifice to a foreign power. At this time Minos, King of Crete, ruled the sea with his fleet of ships. Once he had made war on Athens because his son, a famous wrestler, had been murdered by the Athenians. He refused to make peace except on the condition that every year the Athenians should send him seven young men and seven girls. These, when they arrived in Crete, were to be put inside the famous labyrinth which the great artist Daedalus had built, and then they were to be devoured by the monstrous creature, half man, half bull, which was known as the Minotaur. The Athenians were forced to accept these conditions. Every year the youths and maidens were chosen by lot, and every year, among the lamentations of the whole people, they set out for Crete in a ship which carried black sails as a sign of mourning.

When Theseus heard of this cruel custom he resolved to be himself one of the seven young men who were handed over to Minos. "Either I shall save my people," he said, "or I shall die with them. In any case I shall have done what I can."

His old father Aegeus was reluctant to let him go, but Theseus insisted on the plan which he had made. "Go then," said his father, "and may the gods preserve you! When the time comes I shall watch every day for your return. If you are successful and come back alive, change the sails of your ship to white, so that I may know at once what has happened."

Theseus promised to do as his father had asked him. Then he and the other thirteen victims, girls and young men, said farewell to their city, their friends and their relations and embarked in a black ship with black sails which was to take them to Crete.

When they arrived at the great city of King Minos they looked in astonishment at the huge buildings decorated with paintings in all kinds of colors. There were paintings of bullfights, at which the Cretans were particularly expert, of sea creatures, octopuses, dolphins and twining seaweeds. There were other paintings showing the life of the country —pictures of Cretan officers with their hired Negro troops, of priestesses, naked above the waist, with outstretched arms round which coiled sacred serpents. There were high halls and galleries, enormous buildings; and at the seaport thronged the ships of Egypt and of Asia doing trade with the kingdom of Minos.

Theseus and his companions were, according to the custom, entertained for one night at the palace of the king. On the next day they were to be sent into the intricate mazes of the labyrinth. It was known that there was no escape from this place. The most that anyone could hope for was to die of hunger while wandering in the countless passages before meeting the monstrous Minotaur who would devour any human creature whom he met.

Theseus, as he sat at dinner and told King Minos of the exploits which he had already achieved, won not only the attention but also the love of the king's daughter Ariadne. She could not bear the thought that so beautiful and distinguished a young man should perish miserably on the next day and she determined to help him.

When, therefore, the fourteen young Athenians were led to the entrance of the labyrinth, Ariadne took Theseus aside and put into his hands a ball of wool. "Fasten one end of this wool," she said to him, "inside the doors, and, as you

go, unwind the rest. Then, if you are successful in killing the monster, you will be able to find your way back again. I shall be waiting for you. In return for helping you I want you to take me back with you to Greece and make me your wife."

Theseus readily agreed to do as she said. As well as the ball of wool she had brought him a sword, and, hiding this underneath his cloak, he went forward into the labyrinth. The girls and the other young men waited for him inside the gates, while he picked his way along passages which turned and twisted and linked up with other passages, winding in and out, turning abruptly, or sweeping in long or short curves. As he went he unwound the ball of wool and listened carefully for any noise that might tell him of the whereabouts of the strange monster with whom he was to fight. For long he wandered in complete silence and then, as he approached a part of the labyrinth where the walls turned at right angles, he heard the noise of heavy breathing, a noise that might have been made by an animal or might almost have been made by a man. He put down the ball of wool, gripped his sword in his hand, and advanced cautiously to the corner. Looking round it he saw a monstrous shape. Standing, with his head lowered, was the figure of a giant, but, on the massive neck and shoulders was not a human head but the swinging dewlaps, blunt muzzle and huge horns of a bull. For a moment Theseus and the Minotaur gazed at each other. Then, after pawing the ground with his feet, the monster lowered his head and plunged forward. In the narrow passage Theseus had no room to step aside. With his left hand he seized one of the creature's horns and violently threw the head back while he buried his sword in the thick muscles of its neck. With a roar of pain the Minotaur shook his head and fell backwards. Theseus clung to the beast's throat, avoiding the blows of the great horns, and, stabbing with his sword, soon drenched the floors and walls with blood. The struggle was soon over. Theseus left the great body on the ground and, picking up what was left of the ball of wool, he began to rewind it and so retrace his steps to the place where he had left his companions. Seeing him safe, with the blood upon his hands, they knew that he had been victorious and crowded round him to press his hand and congratulate him upon his victory.

But there was no time to lose. Ariadne was waiting for them and she hid them until nightfall. In the dark they reached their ship, hoisted the sails and escaped. Never more would Athens have to pay the abominable tribute to the King of Crete.

On their return voyage they stopped for the night at the island of Naxos. Here some god put into the hearts and minds of Theseus and his companions a strange and cruel forgetfulness. They rose at dawn and sailed away, leaving Ariadne asleep on the seashore. When she woke and saw the ship far away on the horizon and realized that she had been deserted, she wept and tore her hair, calling all the gods to witness how treacherously she had been treated by the man whose life she had saved. Alone and miserable she wandered on the rocky shore, frightened of wild beasts, but grieving most of all for the loss of her lover.

Here, in her terror, misery and loneliness, she was saved

by the god Bacchus. Tigers and lynxes drew the chariot in which he rode. Behind him came, riding on a mule, his drunken old companion Silenus, with a band of fauns, satyrs and dancing worshipers waving their ivy wands, their loose hair wreathed in ivy or in myrtle. The sand and rocks of the deserted shore grew green with sprouting vines as the procession passed. Ariadne, too, felt the joy of the god's presence. Bacchus loved her and made her his wife. He took the crown that she wore upon her head and set it in the sky as a constellation among the stars.

Meanwhile Theseus sailed on to Athens. The joy and glory of his return was spoiled by another act of forgetfulness. His father Aegeus had told him that, if he returned safe, he was to change the black sails of the ship and hoist white sails as a sign of victory. This Theseus forgot to do, and when his old father, watching from the cliffs, saw a vessel with black sails coming from the south, believing that his son was dead, he threw himself down into the sea. So the day of Theseus's return was a day not only of triumph but of mourning.

Theseus, King of Athens

On the death of Aegeus, Theseus became king of Athens and the surrounding country. His government, both in peace and war, was strong and just, and, though at the end of his life the Athenians showed themselves ungrateful to him, long after his death they gave him the honors due to gods and heroes.

During his reign he saved Athens from two great invasions. First the warlike nation of the Amazons swept over the northern passes and reached the walls of Athens itself. The Amazons were women who spent their lives in fighting. Their power extended over much of Asia, and now their great army entered Greece. These women fought on horseback with javelins and bows. They carried shields shaped like the crescent moon. Led by their queen Hippolyte they had already conquered many armies of men, and, at their approach, the country people deserted their fields and farms, flocking into the city of Athens to escape the ferocity of this host of women. Theseus led his army out against them and for a long time the battle swayed this way and that. The arrows of the Amazons darkened the sky; their horses wheeled and charged again and again upon the Athenian infantry. It was not until, coming to close quarters, Theseus himself fought with the queen of the Amazons, dragged her from her horse and made her prisoner, that the ranks of the Amazons broke. Many of both sides lay dead upon the plain, but the Athenians were victorious. The Amazon army withdrew from Greece. Hippolyte, their queen, became the wife of Theseus and, before she died, gave birth to a son who was called Hippolytus, a strong and noble boy who devoted himself to hunting and to the worship of the goddess Diana.

The next invasion of the land of Athens ended without bloodshed and in a memorable friendship. Pirithous, king of the Lapiths who lived in the north near the country of the centaurs, had heard of the fame of Theseus and decided to see for himself whether he was as brave as he was said to be. So, with a large army, he invaded the country and reached the plain of Marathon where Theseus, at the head of his own army, marched out to meet him. On one side lay the sea and on the other the mountains. The two great hosts were drawn up in order of battle, and both Theseus and Pirithous stood out conspicuous in their armor in front of their men. The two kings looked closely at one another and each was so struck with the beauty and nobility of the other that they immediately laid down their arms and became ever afterwards the most inseparable of friends. Pirithous offered to pay for any damage that his army had done in Attica. Theseus promised him help and alliance for ever in the future. So instead of fighting together the two friends entered Athens in peace and spent many days in feasting and rejoicing.

Not long afterwards Pirithous married a wife who was called Hippodamia. To the wedding feast he invited not only his friend Theseus but all the heroes of Greece. He invited also the centaurs, half men, half horses, who lived on the borders of his territories. Also he invited the gods, but one of them he failed to invite. This was Mars, the god of war.

In anger at being passed over, Mars determined to make the wedding banquet a scene of blood and warfare. One of the centaurs was already drunk with wine and Mars put into his heart the desire to offer violence to the bride. In a drunken fury he attempted to carry Hippodamia away with him; but Theseus immediately killed the insulter of his friend's wife. This was the signal for a general fight. The centaurs sprang up, each on his four legs, and began to attack the Lapiths with arrows and with the short heavy clubs which they carried. The women fled shrieking from the palace and for long the battle raged. Theseus, Pirithous and Hercules were the chief champions on the one side. On the other was a mass of whirling clubs, clattering hooves and great hairy bodies that struggled and twisted in the battle. Finally the centaurs were defeated. With wild cries they fled from the hall and Pirithous with his Lapiths pursued them as they galloped away over the plain to their haunts in the mountains.

Whether because this terrible battle had shocked her too deeply or for some other reason, Hippodamia died soon afterwards. Theseus also had lost his wife and now the two friends determined to find themselves other wives to marry. This was a natural thing to do, but the way in which they did it was both unnatural and wrong.

First they decided to carry off by force the young girl Helen, who much later was to be the cause of the great war at Troy. They seized her from her home in Sparta, and, since she was only ten years old, Theseus put her in the care of his mother Aethra until she should be old enough to marry him. But Helen's two great brothers, Castor and Pollux, soon heard what had happened and rode to Athens to rescue their sister. Theseus had never fought in an unjust war. He knew that what he had done was wrong, and he restored Helen safe and sound to her home.

But the next exploit of Theseus and Pirithous was even more wicked and even less successful. Pirithous actually dared to try to carry off Proserpine, the queen of the lower world and wife of Pluto. Theseus had promised to help his friend in everything and so he accompanied him down to the lower world. Successfully they passed the terrible watchdog Cerberus and advanced into the pale kingdoms of the dead. But both Pluto and Proserpine had been forewarned of their wicked plan which was destined to come to nothing. As they wandered through the murky darkness of the outskirts of Hell, Theseus sat down to rest on a rock. As he did so he felt his limbs change and grow stiff. He tried to rise, but could not. He was fixed to the rock on which he sat. Then as he turned to cry out to his friend Pirithous, he saw that Pirithous was crying out too. Round him were standing the terrible band of Furies, with snakes in their hair, torches and long whips in their hands. Before these monsters the hero's courage failed and by them he was led away to eternal punishment. As he vanished from Theseus's sight, a voice could be heard saying: "From this warning learn wisdom and not to despise the gods."

So for many months in half darkness Theseus sat, immovably fixed to the rock, mourning both for his friend and for himself. In the end he was rescued by Hercules who, coming to Hades to fetch the dog Cerberus, persuaded Proserpine to forgive him for the part he had taken in the rash venture of Pirithous. So Theseus was restored to the upper air, but Pirithous never again left the kingdom of the dead.

Theseus himself was not fated to end his life happily. During the time of his imprisonment in Pluto's kingdom, a usurper, Menestheus, had seized the throne of Athens and driven out the children of Theseus. Partly by bribes and partly by terror he had made himself secure, and, when Theseus returned, his ungrateful people refused to recognize their true king. Theseus was forced to retire into exile in the little island of Scyros, and there he was treacherously murdered by the king of the island, who, while pretending to show his guest the view from the top of a hill, pushed him over a steep precipice.

Many years later, when Athens was known as the great sea power which had conquered Persia, an Athenian admiral came to Scyros and found there in a huge coffin the bones of the great hero. In great state he brought the bones back to Athens, and there ever afterwards the people honored the shrine and temple where the bones were laid.

Orpheus and Eurydice

ORPHEUS, son of one of the Muses, the famous poet and musician, married a wife who was called Eurydice. His marriage brought him no happiness, because while his bride was walking in the deep grass with two of her friends she stepped upon a poisonous snake which bit her in the ankle. She fell to the ground and no skill of any doctor could save her life.

Her friends, the Dryads, wept for her and filled the mountains with their cries. Orpheus himself, sitting solitary on the seashore, from daybreak to sunset mourned for his wife to the sad music of his lyre. He even dared to descend to the lower world where the insubstantial ghosts flit to and fro, the terrible kingdom of Proserpine. At the sound of the music of his lyre the ghosts came thronging in crowds like the flocks of birds that nightfall or a sudden winter shower drives down from the mountains to roost among the leaves of trees. There were mothers and fathers, the dead spirits of great heroes, boys and unmarried girls, young men who had died early and been placed on their funeral pyres before their parents' eyes. All these were penned in by the dark muddy banks of the slow rivers of Hell with their ugly reeds, the river Cocytus and the river Styx which folds in the ghosts with its nine sweeping circles. Not only these spirits, but the very prison house and torture chambers of the dead were lulled to rest by the music of Orpheus. The Furies themselves, with the snakes twined in their hair, stood still, and for the first and only time their cheeks were wet with tears. Tantalus forgot to put his lips to the water that always escaped him; the vulture paused above the giant body of Tityus and no longer pecked at his liver; the wheel where Ixion was tortured stood still; the Belides put down their pitchers, and Sisyphus sat down on the rock that he was condemned for ever to push uphill.

Orpheus stood before Proserpine and her husband, the terrible King Pluto. Still striking music from his lyre he spoke to them: "Powers of the lower world, to whom all of us who are mortal must come in the end, let me speak to you sincerely and tell you the truth. I have not come here as a robber or to vex you in your kingdom. The reason I have come here is my wife. A serpent bit her and took away her life just as she was growing up. I tried to bear her loss, but I cannot. Love is too strong for me. In the world above, Love is a well-known god: whether he is known here also I do not know, but I think that he must be and, if the old story is true, you also were joined together by Love. I pray you therefore, by the fearful silence of your vast kingdom, give me back Eurydice, give her back the life that was so quickly taken from her. In the end we shall all come to you. This is our final home, and you rule the longest over the race of men. Eurydice too, sooner or later, will come back to you. Now I ask you as a gift to allow me to enjoy her for a little time. If the Fates will not allow this, then I have decided not to return myself, and you may rejoice in the death of us both."

Proserpine and Pluto were touched by his words and by his music. They could not refuse his request and they called for Eurydice. She was among the ghosts who had only just arrived and she came still limping from the wound in her foot.

Orpheus then received his wife back, but only on the condition that he should go in front of her and not turn his eyes backwards until he had ascended the steep path from the lower world and had reached the upper air.

So, through thick dark mist, in the tremendous silence of Hades, they took the steep path, and they were already close to the borders of the upper world, when there swept over the mind of Orpheus, in his love and fear for Eurydice, a sudden madness, something which might, one would have thought, have been forgiven him, if only the powers below knew how to forgive. Now all his toil was in vain. He had broken the conditions which savage Pluto had made and three times came the crash of thunder from the lakes and rivers of Hell. Eurydice cried to him: "O Orpheus what is this madness which has betrayed us both? O see, the cruel fates are calling for me again, and sleep is falling over my swimming eyes. Farewell, O Orpheus. Still I stretch out to you my feeble hands, but I am yours no longer. I am being pulled away from you, and all round me is the vastness of night."

As she spoke she melted away suddenly from his sight and disappeared like smoke disappears into thin air. Eagerly he stretched out his arms to embrace her, but his arms encountered nothing that could be touched. He spoke to her, but there was no one to listen to him, nor would the guards of the lower world allow him to cross again the river that separated him from the dead. On that river Eurydice, already cold in death, was sailing back again to the abodes of the ghosts.

For seven months they say that Orpheus sang to his lyre in the rocky places, lamenting his wife twice lost to him. But however rocky the place, there was soon shade there; for the trees hurried to hear his music—oaks and ashes, firs, poplars, all the trees of the woods, with vines also, ivy and climbing plants. All beasts and birds came too, to listen to him. There were tigers and cattle together, wolves and sheep, eagles and trembling doves. So Orpheus continued to sing, in pain for the loss of his wife, as the nightingale in the thick leaves of a poplar sings in pain for the loss of her brood which some rough plowman has seen and taken from their nest before they can fly: meanwhile the mother bird mourns throughout the night and, sitting on a branch, starts again and again her sad song, and in all the country around, one hears her piercing notes. So Orpheus sang, soothing the fierce hearts of tigers, and drawing trees after him.

In all this time he gave no thought to women, though

many women loved him and wished to be married to him. At last, they say, a band of women, driven wild by their dancing in the mountains by night, and angry at being despised by him, swept down upon the divine singer and tore him limb from limb, scattering the fragments of his body far and wide throughout the fields of Thrace. As for his head, wrenched from the neck that was as white as marble, the river Hebrus carried it to the sea and across the sea to the island of Lesbos. And, as the head was rolled in the river's stream, the voice and cold tongue still cried: "Eurydice, my poor Eurydice!" and the name Eurydice was echoed from the banks.

The fragments of his body were collected together for burial and in the Thracian town where his tomb is, the nightingales still sing with greater beauty than in any other place. His spirit went below the earth and, on its last journey, recognized all the surroundings which it had visited before. Searching through the Elysian fields where the blessed spirits are, he found Eurydice and caught her in his arms. Now they wander there together; sometimes they walk side by side, sometimes he follows her, sometimes he goes in front and now can safely look back at her with no fear of ever losing her again.

The Labors of Hercules

HERCULES suffered much during his life, but after his death he became a god. His mother was Alcmena, his father was Jupiter, and he was the strongest of all the heroes who lived in his time.

All through his life he was pursued by the hatred and jealousy of Juno who tried to destroy him even in his cradle. She sent two great snakes to attack the sleeping baby, but Hercules awoke, grasped their necks in his hands and strangled them both.

Before he was eighteen he had done many famous deeds in the country of Thebes, and Creon, the king, gave him his daughter in marriage. But he could not long escape the anger of Juno, who afflicted him with a sudden madness, so that he did not know what he was doing and in a fit of frenzy killed both his wife and his children. When he came to his senses, in horror and shame at what he had done, he visited the great cliffs of Delphi, where the eagles circle all day and where Apollo's oracle is. There he asked how he could be purified of his sin and he was told by the oracle that he must go to Mycenae and for twelve years obey all the commands of the cowardly king Eurystheus, his kinsman. It seemed a hard and cruel sentence, but the oracle told him also that at the end of many labors he would be received among the gods.

Hercules therefore departed to the rocky citadel of Mycenae that looks down upon the blue water of the bay of Argos. He was skilled in the use of every weapon, having been educated, as Jason was, by the wise centaur Chiron. He was tall and immensely powerful. When Eurystheus saw him he was both terrified of him and jealous of his great powers. He began to devise labors that would seem impossible, yet Hercules accomplished them all.

First he was ordered to destroy and to bring back to Mycenae the lion of Nemea, which for long had ravaged all the countryside to the north. Hercules took his bow and arrows, and, in the forest of Nemea, cut himself a great club, so heavy that a man nowadays could hardly lift it. This club he carried ever afterwards as his chief weapon.

He found that his arrows had no effect on the tough skin of the lion, but, as the beast sprang at him, he half stunned it with his club; then, closing in with it, he seized it by the throat and killed it with his bare hands. They say that when he carried back on his shoulders to Mycenae the body of the huge beast, Eurystheus fled in terror and ordered Hercules never again to enter the gates of the city, but to wait outside until he was told to come in. Eurystheus also built for himself a special strong room of brass into which he would retire if he was ever again frightened by the power and valiance of Hercules. Hercules himself took the skin of the lion and made it into a cloak which he wore ever afterwards, sometimes with the lion's head covering his own head like a cap, sometimes with it slung backwards over his shoulders.

The next task given to Hercules by Eurystheus was to destroy a huge water snake, called the Hydra, which lived in the marshes of Argos, was filled with poison and had fifty venomous heads. Hercules, with his friend and companion, the young Iolaus, set out from Mycenae and came to the great cavern, sacred to Pan, which is a holy place in the hills near Argos. Below this cavern a river gushes out of the rock. Willows and plane trees surround the source and the brilliant green of grass. It is the freshest and most delightful place. But, as the river flows downwards to the sea, it becomes wide and shallow, extending into pestilential marshes, the home of stinging flies and mosquitoes. In these marshes they found the Hydra, and Hercules, with his great club, began to crush the beast's heads, afterwards cutting them off with his sword. Yet the more he labored, the more difficult his task became. From the stump of each head that he cut off, two other heads, with forked and hissing tongues, immediately sprang. Faced with an endless and increasing effort, Hercules was at a loss what to do. It seemed to him that heat might prove more powerful than cold steel, and he commanded Iolaus to burn the root of each head with a red-hot iron immediately it was severed from the neck. This plan was successful. The heads no longer sprouted up again, and soon the dangerous and destructive animal lay dead, though still writhing in the black marsh water among the reeds. Hercules cut its body open and dipped his arrows in the blood. Henceforward these arrows would bring certain death, even if they only grazed the skin, so powerful was the Hydra's poison.

Eurystheus next ordered Hercules to capture and bring back alive a stag, sacred to Diana and famous for its great fleetness of foot, which lived in the waste mountains and forests, and never yet had been approached in the chase. For a whole year Hercules pursued this animal, resting for the hours of darkness and pressing on next day in its tracks. For many months he was wholly outdistanced; valleys and forests divided him from his prey. But at the end of the year the stag, weary of the long hunt, could run no longer. Hercules seized it in his strong hands, tied first its forelegs and then its hind legs together, put the body of the beast, with its drooping antlered head, over his neck, and proceeded to return to the palace of King Eurystheus. However, as he was on his way through the woods, he was suddenly aware of a bright light in front of him, and in the middle of the light he saw standing a tall woman or, as he immediately recognized, a goddess, grasping in her hands a bow and staring at him angrily with her shining eyes. He knew at once that this was the archer goddess Diana, she who had once turned Actaeon into a stag and who now was enraged at the loss of this other stag which was sacred to her. Hercules put his prey on the ground and knelt before the goddess. "It was through no desire of my own," he said, "that I have captured this noble animal. What I do is done at the command of my father Jupiter and of the oracle of your brother Apollo at Delphi." The goddess listened to his explanation, smiled kindly on him and allowed him to go on his way, when he had promised that, once the stag had been carried to Eurystheus, it would be set free again in the forests that it loved. So Hercules accomplished this third labor.

He was not, however, to be allowed to rest. Eurystheus now commanded him to go out to the mountains of Erymanthus and bring back the great wild boar that for long had terrorized all the neighborhood. So Hercules set out once more and on his way he passed the country where the centaurs had settled after they had been driven down from the north in the battle that had taken place with the Lapiths at the wedding of Pirithous. In this battle they had already had experience of the hero's strength, but still their manners were rude and rough. When the centaur Pholus offered Hercules some of their best wine to drink, the other centaurs became jealous. Angry words led to blows, and soon Hercules was forced to defend himself with his club and with his arrows, the poison of which not only caused death, but also the most extreme pain. Soon he scattered his enemies in all directions, driving them over the plains and rocks. Some he dashed to the ground with his club; others, wounded by the poisoned arrows, lay writhing in agony, or kicking their hooves in the air. Some took refuge in the house of the famous centaur Chiron, who had been schoolmaster to Hercules and who, alone among the centaurs, was immortal. As he pursued his enemies to this good centaur's house, shooting arrows at them as he went, Hercules, by an unhappy accident, wounded Chiron himself. Whether it was because of grief that his old pupil had so injured him, or whether it was because of the great pain of the wound, Chiron prayed to Jupiter that his immortality should be taken away from him. Jupiter granted his prayer. The good centaur died, but he was set in Heaven in a constellation of stars which is still called either Sagittarius or else The Centaur.

Hercules mourned the sad death of his old master. Then he went on to Erymanthus. It was winter and he chased the great boar up to the deep snow in the passes of the mountains. The animal's short legs soon grew weary of plowing through the stiff snow and Hercules caught it up when it was exhausted and panting in a snowdrift. He bound it firmly and slung the great body over his back. They say that when he brought it to Mycenae, Eurystheus was so frightened at the sight of the huge tusks and flashing eyes that he hid for two days in the brass hiding place that he had had built for him.

The next task that Hercules was ordered to do would have seemed to anyone impossible. There was a king of Elis called Augeas, very rich in herds of goats and cattle. His stables, they say, held three thousand oxen and for ten years these stables had never been cleaned. The dung and muck stood higher than a house, hardened and caked together. The smell was such that even the herdsmen, who were used to it, could scarcely bear to go near. Hercules was now ordered to clean these stables, and, going to Elis, he first asked the king to promise him the tenth part of his herds if he was successful in his task. The king readily agreed, and Hercules made the great river Alpheus change his course and come foaming and roaring through the filthy stables. In less than a day all the dirt was cleared and rolled away to the sea. The river then went back to its former course and, for the first time in ten years, the stone floors and walls of the enormous stables shone white and clean.

Hercules then asked for his reward, but King Augeas, claiming that he had performed the task not with his own hands, but by a trick, refused to give it to him. He even banished his own son, who took the side of Hercules and reproached his father for not keeping his promise. Hercules then made war on the kingdom of Elis, drove King Augeas out and put his son on the throne. Then, with his rich reward, he returned to Mycenae, ready to undertake whatever new task was given him by Eurystheus.

Again he was ordered to destroy creatures that were harmful to men. This time they were great birds, like cranes or storks, but much more powerful, which devoured human flesh and lived around the black waters of the Stymphalian lake. In the reeds and rocky crags they lived in huge numbers and Hercules was at a loss how to draw them from their hiding places. It was the goddess Minerva who helped him by giving him a great rattle of brass. The noise of this rattle drove the great birds into the air in throngs. Hercules pursued them with his arrows, which rang upon their horny beaks and legs but stuck firm in the bodies that tumbled one after the other into the lake. The whole brood of these monsters was entirely destroyed and now only ducks and harmless waterfowl nest along the reedy shores.

Hercules had now accomplished six of his labors. Six more remained. After the killing of the Stymphalian birds he was commanded to go to Crete and bring back from there alive a huge bull which was laying the whole island waste. Barehanded and alone he grappled with this bull, and, once again, when he brought the animal back into the streets of Mycenae, Eurystheus fled in terror at the sight both of the hero and of the great beast which he had captured.

From the southern sea Hercules was sent to the north to Thrace, over which ruled King Diomedes, a strong and warlike prince who savagely fed his famous mares on human flesh. Hercules conquered the king in battle and gave his body to the very mares which had so often fed upon the bodies of the king's enemies. He brought the mares back to King Eurystheus, who again was terrified at the sight of such fierce and spirited animals. He ordered them to be taken to the heights of Mount Olympus and there be consecrated to Jupiter. But Jupiter had no love for these unnatural creatures, and, on the rocky hillsides, they were devoured by lions, wolves and bears.

Next Hercules was commanded to go to the country of the Amazons, the fierce warrior women, and bring back the girdle of their queen Hippolyte. Seas and mountains had to be crossed, battles to be fought; but Hercules in the end accomplished the long journey and the dangerous task. Later, as is well known, Hippolyte became the wife of Theseus of Athens and bore him an ill-fated son, Hippolytus.

Hercules had now traveled in the south, the north and the east. His tenth labor was to be in the far west, beyond the country of Spain, in an island called Erythia. Here lived the giant Geryon, a great monster with three bodies and three heads. With his herdsman, and his two-headed dog, called Orthrus, he looked after huge flocks of oxen, and, at the command of Eurystheus, Hercules came into his land to lift the cattle and to destroy the giant. On his way, at the very entrance to the Atlantic he set up two great marks, ever afterwards to be known by sailors and called the Pillars of Hercules. Later, as he wandered through rocks and over desert land, he turned his anger against the Sun itself, shooting his arrows at the great god Phoebus Apollo. But Phoebus pitied him in his thirst and weariness. He sent him a golden boat, and in this boat Hercules crossed over to the island of Erythia. Here he easily destroyed both watchdog and herdsman, but fought for long with the great three-bodied giant before he slew him, body after body. Then he began to drive the cattle over rivers and mountains and deserts from Spain to Greece. As he was passing through Italy he came near the cave where Cacus, a son of Vulcan, who breathed fire out of his mouth, lived solitary and cruel, since he killed all strangers and nailed their heads, dripping with blood, to the posts at the entrance of his rocky dwelling. While Hercules was resting, with the herds all round him, Cacus came out of his cave and stole eight of the best animals of the whole herd. He dragged them backwards by their tails, so that Hercules should not be able to track them down.

When Hercules awoke from his rest, he searched far and wide for the missing animals, but, since they had been driven into the deep recesses of Cacus's cave, he was unable to find them. In the end he began to go on his way with the rest of the herd, and, as the stolen animals heard the lowing of the other cattle, they too began to low and bellow in their rocky prison. Hercules stopped still, and soon out of the cave came the fire-breathing giant, prepared to defend the fruits of his robbery and anxious to hang the head of Hercules among his other disgusting trophies. This, however, was not to be. The huge limbs and terrible fiery breath of Cacus were of no avail against the hero's strength and fortitude. Soon, with a tremendous blow of his club, he stretched out Cacus dead on the ground. Then he drove the great herd on over mountains and plains, through forests and rivers to Mycenae.

Hercules' next labor again took him to the far west. He was commanded by Eurystheus to fetch him some of the golden apples of the Hesperides. These apples grew in a garden west even of the land of Atlas. Here the sun shines continually, but always cool well-watered trees of every kind give shade. All flowers and fruits that grow on earth grow here, and fruit and flowers are always on the boughs together. In the center of the garden is the orchard where golden apples gleam among the shining green leaves and the flushed blossom. Three nymphs, the Hesperides, look after this orchard, which was given by Jupiter to Juno as a wedding present. It is guarded also by a great dragon that never sleeps, and coils its huge folds around the trees. No one except the gods knows exactly where this beautiful and remote garden is, and it was to this unknown place that Hercules was sent.

He was helped by Minerva and by the nymphs of the broad river Po in Italy. These nymphs told Hercules where to find Nereus, the ancient god of the sea, who knew the past, the present and the future. "Wait for him," they said, "until you find him asleep on the rocky shore, surrounded by his fifty daughters. Seize hold of him tightly and do not let go until he answers your question. He will, in trying to escape you, put on all kinds of shapes. He will turn to fire, to water, to a wild beast or to a serpent. You must not lose your courage, but hold him all the tighter, and, in the end, he will come back to his own shape and will tell you what you want to know."

Hercules followed their advice. As he watched along the sea god's shore he saw, lying on the sand, half in and half out of the sea, with seaweed trailing round his limbs, the old god himself. Around him were his daughters, the Nereids, some riding on the backs of dolphins, some dancing on the shore, some swimming and diving in the deeper water. As Hercules approached, they cried out shrilly at the sight of a man. Those on land leaped back into the sea; those in the sea swam further from the shore. But their cries did not awake their father till Hercules was close to him and able to grip him firmly in his strong hands. Immediately the old god felt the hands upon him, his body seemed to disappear into a running stream of water; but Hercules felt the body that he could not see, and did not relax his grasp. Next it seemed that his hands were buried in a great pillar of fire; but the fire did not scorch the skin and Hercules could still feel the aged limbs through the fire. Then it was a great lion with wide-open jaws that appeared to be lying and raging on the sands; then a bear, then a dragon. Still Hercules clung firmly to his prisoner, and in the end he saw again the bearded face and seaweed-dripping limbs of old Nereus. The god knew for what purpose Hercules had seized him, and he told him the way to the garden of the Hesperides.

It was a long and difficult journey, but at the end of it Hercules was rewarded. The guardian nymphs (since this was the will of Jupiter) allowed him to pick from the pliant boughs two or three of the golden fruit. The great dragon bowed its head to the ground at their command and left Hercules unmolested. He brought back the apples to Eurystheus, but soon they began to lose that beautiful sheen of gold that had been theirs in the western garden. So Minerva carried them back again to the place from which they came, and then once more they glowed with their own gold among the other golden apples that hung upon the trees.

Now had come the time for the twelfth and last of the labors that Hercules did for his master Eurystheus. This labor would seem to anyone by far the hardest; for the hero was commanded to descend into the lower world, and bring back with him from the kingdom of Proserpine the terrible three-headed watchdog Cerberus.

Hercules took the dark path which before him had been trodden only by Orpheus and Theseus and Pirithous.

Orpheus had returned. Theseus and Pirithous, for their wicked attempt, were still imprisoned.

Hercules passed the Furies, undaunted by the frightful eyes beneath the writhing serpents of their hair. He passed the great criminals, Sisyphus, Tantalus and the rest. He passed by his friend, the unhappy Theseus, who was sitting immovably fixed to a rock, and he came at last into the terrible presence of black Pluto himself, who sat on his dark throne with his young wife Proserpine beside him. To the King and Queen of the Dead, Hercules explained the reason of his coming. "Go," said Pluto, "and, so long as you use no weapon, but only your bare hands, you may take my watchdog Cerberus to the upper air."

Hercules thanked the dreadful king for giving him the permission which he had asked. Then he made one more request which was that Theseus, who had sinned only by keeping his promise to his friend, might be allowed to return again to life. This, too, was granted him. Theseus rose to his feet again and accompanied the hero to the entrance of Hell, where the huge dog Cerberus, with his three heads and his three deep baying voices, glared savagely at the intruders. Even this tremendous animal proved no match for Hercules, who with his vice-like grip stifled the breath in two of the shaggy throats, then lifted the beast upon his shoulders and began to ascend again, Theseus following close behind, the path that leads to the world of men. They say that when he carried Cerberus to Mycenae, Eurystheus fled in terror to another city and was now actually glad that Hercules had completed what might seem to have been twelve impossible labors. Cerberus was restored to his place in Hell and never again visited the upper world. Nor did Hercules ever go down to the place of the dead, since, after further trials, he was destined to live among the gods above.

The Death of Hercules

MANY more great deeds, too many to tell, were done by Hercules before the end of his life among men. But he was unfortunate in his love for women.

His first wife, Megara, he had killed in a fit of madness. Then, when he had finished his labors, he wished to marry Iole, daughter of the famous archer, King Eurytus, who had made it known that he would give his daughter in marriage to the man who could defeat him and his three sons in a shooting match. This Hercules did; but King Eurytus, either because he was angry at losing his reputation for archery, or because he remembered the fate of Megara and feared for his own daughter, refused to keep his promise. Hercules departed in anger, vowing revenge. Later, indeed, he had his revenge, but, in having it, he brought upon himself his own fate.

Since he could not have Iole as his wife, he became the suitor of Deianira, daughter of the King of Calydon and sister to Meleager. Many other heroes wished to marry this beautiful girl, but among them all stood out Hercules himself and the great river god Achelous, whose stream runs through the country of Calydon. Each of these two claimed the right to marry Deianira, Hercules because he was the son of Jupiter and had accomplished the twelve labors of which all the world was speaking, Achelous because he was a god and because mortals should give way to gods. "As for Hercules," he said, "he is a foreigner, whereas my river flows through Calydon. As for his father Jupiter, all we know is that Juno hates him and drives him mad. I do not believe that Jupiter is his father at all."

So Achelous spoke, and, while he was speaking, Hercules kept staring at him with fierce eyes beneath his lowering brows. Finally, unable to control his anger, he said: "My hand is better than my tongue. You may conquer me in words, but not in fair fight."

So threatening, he approached Achelous, who after his boastful speeches, was ashamed not to resist him. He threw aside his green clothes, and the two made ready to wrestle, rubbing sand over their bodies, so that the grip of each on each might be firmer. Then they rushed together and Hercules caught now at the river god's neck, now at his waist, now at his knees. But Achelous, with his great weight, stood firm like a huge breakwater against which wave after roaring wave beats in vain. After a time they drew apart, and then rushed together again, each planted firmly in his tracks, determined not to give in. Foot was locked with foot: the straining breasts heaved against each other: fingers were knitted together in the struggle, and forehead pressed against forehead.

Three times, with enormous effort, but in vain, did Her-

cules try to thrust away from him the weight of the breast
that pressed on his. Finally he broke away from the hold,
knocked Achelous sideways with a blow from his fist and
sprang upon his back. To the river god it seemed that he
was carrying a mountain. His arms were pouring with
sweat as he tried to loosen the fierce grip of his antagonist.
Hercules gave him no chance to recover his strength, but,
bearing down upon his neck, forced him, gasping for
breath, to touch the ground with his knees.

Never before had the god been overthrown, and,
now knowing that he could never conquer Hercules by
strength, he attempted to conquer him by magic tricks. He
changed his body and slipped out of Hercules' grasp in the
form of a long snake, which wound itself into great coils,
reared up and darted out its forked tongue in savage hissing. Hercules merely laughed. "Achelous," he said, "I used
to kill snakes when I was in my cradle. And as for you,
with your one head, think of the Hydra of Lerna, with its
hundred ever-growing heads. I killed that monster, and
what do you think will become of you, who are not really
a snake at all?"

So he spoke, and fastened his tremendous grip on the
neck of the false serpent, till, half throttled, the river god
knew that in this shape also he was conquered. There was
one more thing that he could do. He turned himself into
a bull, and fought in that shape. But Hercules flung his
arms round the bull's neck and dragged it down as it tried
to run. He pressed the hard horns right down to the earth
and overthrew the great body in the deep sand. Not content with this he tore off one of the horns from the fore-

head. This horn the nymphs took and filled with fruit and sweet-smelling flowers, making it a holy horn. Now it is carried by the glad goddess Abundance. But Achelous retired to his own stream. In his real shape he used to have two small horns on his head. Now he had lost one of them, and attempted to disguise the loss by covering the empty space with leaves of willow and with reeds.

Hercules now had won Deianira for his wife. But while he was on his way home with her, he came to the swift stream of the river Evenus, which, swollen by winter storms, was higher than usual, full of whirling eddies and hard indeed to pass. While Hercules stood on the bank, with no fear for himself but frightened for his young wife, the centaur Nessus came up to him. Nessus knew the fords well and was himself strong of limb. "Let me," he said, "carry your wife across the river, Hercules. You, with your great strength, can swim across."

Hercules agreed. He threw his club and his bow over to the other side, and then, just as he was, with his lion skin and his quiver, he plunged into the roaring water, breasted it strongly and reached the further bank. There, as he was picking up his bow, he heard his wife's voice crying out, and, looking round, saw that the treacherous centaur was trying to carry her away. "Nessus you thief," he cried out, "you who have dared to touch what belongs to me, have no faith in your four horse's legs. If not my feet, then my arrows will overtake you." The thing was no sooner said than done. He shot an arrow at the fleeing centaur. It struck him in the back and the point came out through his breast. Nessus tore the arrow out of the wound and there followed a stream of blood all infected with the deadly poison of the Hydra. The blood soaked through the tunic which he wore, and Nessus, on the point of death saying to himself, "I shall not die unavenged," gave the tunic to Deianira, telling her that, if ever her husband should cease to love her, this tunic would prove a powerful charm to bring back his love.

After this many years went by, and the fame of the deeds of Hercules had filled the earth. In the end he made war on King Eurytus, who once had refused him Iole. He conquered him in battle and took his family prisoner. On his way home he came to Mount Oeta, and there he prepared to sacrifice to his father Jupiter. First, however, he sent his servant Lichas to Deianira, asking her to give him clean clothes for the sacrifice. Meanwhile, however, Rumor, which exaggerates everything, had been busy. Deianira had been told that Hercules had once again fallen deeply in love with Iole, whom he was bringing home with him as a captive. Deianira believed this story and, in her love for Hercules, was terrified by it. First she burst into tears of agony and self-pity. Then she said to herself: "Why should I cry? This other woman would be glad to think of me crying. I must think of some plan worthy of the sister of Meleager."

Many ideas occurred to her, but in the end what seemed best was to send to Hercules the blood-soaked tunic which Nessus had given her so long ago, and which, she thought, would make her husband love her again. So she gave the tunic to Lichas, who little knew what he was carrying. She herself also sent kind messages, and had no knowledge that she was destroying both her husband and herself. Hercules, all unsuspecting, took the gift and put on his body the poison of the Hydra.

Then, as the flames began to leap up on the altars, as he was praying, with the incense curling in smoke from the flames, suddenly from the heat of his body the violence of the poison was aroused and began to spread like fire over his limbs. So long as he could do so, he kept back his groans, forcing down the pain with his strong and resolute mind. But when the pain was past endurance, he threw the altar down and filled the forests of Oeta with his cries. He tried to tear the deadly tunic from his body, but it stuck to his flesh and, where he tore it away, he tore away also his own skin, laying bare veins and huge muscles and strong bones. His very blood boiled and hissed with the poison, as when red-hot iron is put into cold water. Flames spread into every corner of his body, and, in his agony, he raised his hands to heaven and cried out: "O Juno, now you may feed your cruel heart with my sufferings. Are they not enough to be pitied even by an enemy? Will you not take away my life? It was born for toil. Now let it go."

He spoke and again was overcome by pain. As a bull, with the shaft of a weapon sticking in its neck, roars and tosses its head, though the giver of the wound has fled, so Hercules raged along the ridges of Oeta, struggling to rip off his garments, tearing up great trees, and stretching out his arms to his father's heaven.

Suddenly he noticed the trembling Lichas, who was hiding himself in the hollow of a rock. On this his suffering

all turned to the madness of anger. "Was it you, Lichas,"
he said, "who brought this gift that is killing me?"

The young man trembled and grew pale. He began to
make excuses for his ignorance, but while he was still
speaking Hercules seized hold of him, whirled him three
or four times round his head and hurled him out over the
sea, like a bolt sent from a catapult. While still in mid-air
the boy's body began to grow hard. Fear had dried up his
blood, and, just as rain in a cold wind is said to change first
to snow and then to hard hail, so, hurled by those strong
arms through the air, the body of Lichas changed to rock
and as rock fell into the Euboean sea. To this day there
rises where he fell a rock of human shape, and, as though
it was still able to feel, the sailors refuse to step upon it,
and they call it Lichas.

Deianira too had had no knowledge of what she had
done when she sent the fatal garment to Hercules. But
soon messengers came to her with the news of what was
happening, how her husband was being torn to pieces by
the poison and was dead or dying. In bitter remorse and
anguish Deianira put an end to her own life, calling the
gods to witness that what she had desired was not her husband's death but his love.

And now Hercules himself cut down the trees on high
Oeta, and with their trunks made a great funeral pyre.
He was aided by his friend Philoctetes, who lit the pyre
and to whom, as a reward, Hercules gave the famous bow
which later was to go to Troy. Now, at the point of death,
with burned and withered flesh, Hercules grew calm again.
On top of the pyre he spread the skin of the Nemean lion.

He rested his head on his club as on a pillow, and lay down among the flames with peaceful face, as if, after cups of fine wine and crowned with garlands, he were lying on a couch at a banquet.

The gods from heaven looked down and saw that the defender of the earth was dying. Even Juno at last pitied him, and to all the gods and goddesses Jupiter spoke: "Fear not. Hercules has conquered everything, and he will conquer those flames. Part of him is immortal, and, as an immortal, he will live with the gods for ever."

So indeed it happened. As a snake changes its old skin, so Hercules, as the flames consumed his body, seemed to put on a new body, stronger, more heroic, more beautiful and more stately even than before. Thunder pealed, and through the hollow clouds Jupiter sent his four-horsed chariot which bore him to Heaven, where he was welcomed among the shining stars and in the assembly of the gods.

Cephalus and Procris

CEPHALUS, Prince of Thessaly, married Procris, the daughter of Erectheus, King of Athens, and came to live in his wife's country. Both their love and their beauty were equal, and they were rightly called happy. But, two months after the marriage, when Cephalus was hunting deer on the slopes of flowery Hymettus, Aurora, the golden goddess of the Dawn, having just put the darkness to flight, saw the young man and was at once fascinated by his beauty. She snatched him away from earth and took him up to heaven, wishing that he might live with her for ever. Yet in her golden house, full of rosy light, Cephalus thought and talked only of Procris and of the joys of his life with her. The goddess grew angry with him and said, "Stop complaining, you ungrateful man! You can have your Procris. But, if I have any gift of seeing the future, you will end by wishing you had not had her."

So, in anger, she sent Cephalus back to earth. At first he longed only to see his wife, but, as he drew near to Athens, and thought of the goddess's warning, he began to wonder whether Procris had been faithful to him in his absence. She was beautiful and she was young. He knew the goodness of her character, but he had been absent a long time; he had discovered that even goddesses are faithless and then also people who are in love are apt to fear everything. He decided to disguise himself and so try to discover whether his wife was true to him. Aurora helped him in this and made his appearance different from what it had been.

So he entered the city of Athens and, unrecognized, came to his own house. Here he found everything in order, and when, with much difficulty, he had reached the presence of Procris, the sight of her sadness and of her beauty almost made him give up his plan. She was weeping in longing for her lost husband, and Cephalus too longed to tell her who he was and to kiss her, as he ought to have done. However, he went on in the way that he had planned and over and over again offered her great gifts if she would love him. Over and over again she replied: "There is only one man whom I love. Wherever he is, I keep myself for him alone."

Anyone of any sense would have been satisfied with such proofs of faithfulness, but Cephalus continued to offer her great fortunes and enormous gifts. In the end she seemed to hesitate, and then, throwing off his disguise, and appearing in his true form, he cried out: "False wife, it is I, your husband, who was tempting you. I myself am the evidence of your unfaithfulness."

Procris said not a word. Silently and with bowed head she fled from the treachery of her house and of her husband. Hating him and the whole race of men, she wandered in the woods and mountains of Euboea, hunting beasts in the company of Diana and the nymphs.

But, as soon as she had gone, Cephalus became on fire with love for her. He regretted his cruel trick, asked her pardon and confessed that he also, in the same position, would have acted in the same way. Then Procris came back to him and for many years they lived together in perfect happiness, each equally loving the other.

Procris, when she returned to her husband, gave him two gifts which she herself had received from Diana. One was a wonderful hound, called Hurricane, which ran faster than any hound in the world: one was a javelin which always went straight to its mark and then, covered with blood, returned to the hand that had hurled it. Each of these gifts has a story. The story of the javelin is a sad one; the story of the hound is strange.

A monster came into the land of Thebes, killing the cattle and driving the country people into the towns away from their crops. Cephalus, together with the young men of Thebes and of Athens, set out to hunt the beast. They spread their hunting nets, but the fierce animal easily leaped over the top of them. They unleashed their hounds and set them on the track, but the hounds were quickly outdistanced. Then all the hunters called on Cephalus to let Hurricane go from the leash. All the time the hound had been straining forward and struggling to get its neck loose from the strap. Now, no sooner was he let go than he seemed to disappear from sight. His footprints were there in the hot sand, but the dog had sped off faster than an arrow or a sling stone. The hunters climbed to the top of a hill and saw far away in the plain the hound and the animal that it was pursuing close together. At each moment it seemed that the hound would fasten its teeth in the animal's flanks, but then the animal would turn and twist, and the teeth would snap on empty air. Still the hound followed step for step; still the animal barely escaped.

Cephalus took his javelin. For a moment, while he was fitting his fingers into the loop, he turned his head aside, and when he looked back to the plain, he saw a strange sight. Two marble statues stood there, the one appearing to escape, the other to be seizing upon its prey. Some god must have willed that it should be so, that neither of the two should be conquered by the other.

But it was the javelin that brought to Cephalus his great sorrow and ended the happy years in which he and Procris loved each other fully and so much that she would not have taken Jupiter himself instead of her husband, nor could he have been taken from her, not even by the goddess Venus.

Every day in the morning Cephalus used to go hunting in the woods. He went by himself, with no companions and no hounds. His javelin, which never missed its mark, was enough. When he had had enough of hunting, he would go back to the cool shade and the gentle breeze that blows along the cold valleys. The name of the breeze was "Aura," and Cephalus, tired of the heat and the chase, got into the habit of talking to the breeze as though it was a real person. "Come, Aura," he used to say, "come, you sweet thing! Come and refresh me! Come and relieve the heat in which I burn." Or else he would say: "You, Aura, are my chief joy. You comfort and refresh me. You make me love the woods and lonely places. How I love to feel your breath upon my cheek!"

Someone heard Cephalus speaking like this and thought that he must be speaking to some nymph whose name was "Aura," and must certainly be in love with her. The rash informer, so quick at leaping to the wrong conclusions, went to Procris and whispered to her what he had heard. Love will believe anything, and Procris, as Cephalus found out later, fainted away in pain when she heard the story. When she came to herself she lamented her own fate and her husband's unfaithfulness, anxious over something which did not exist, a mere name without a body, just as if it had been a real person and a rival for her love. Still, in all her misery, she often hoped that she was deceived in what she thought, and said to herself that she would not believe it, unless she saw it with her own eyes.

Next day, when dawn rose, Cephalus left his house and went to the woods to hunt. He killed the beasts which he pursued, then, as he often did, he lay down on the grass and said: "Come to me, Aura! Come and soothe me after my exercise!" As he was speaking he thought he heard from somewhere near at hand a moaning sound. But he went on: "Come, dearest!" and then, hearing distinctly something rustling in the leaves and thinking that it was some beast, he hurled his javelin into the thicket.

It was Procris that was hiding there. With a deep wound in her breast she cried out: "Alas! Alas!" At the sound of his faithful wife's voice Cephalus, half out of his mind, rushed to the place from which the voice had come. He found her dying, with the blood pouring over her torn dress, trying to drag out from the wound the very javelin which she had given him as a present. Gently he lifted up the body that was dearer to him than his own; cutting a piece from her dress he bound up the wound and tried to stop the flow of blood, begging her not to leave him with the guilt of having killed her. But now her strength began to fail her. Still, though she was at the point of death, she forced herself to say: "Cephalus, I beg and pray you by our marriage, by all the gods, by all that I have done for you, by our love together, the love which I still feel for you now I am dying, and which caused my death, do not let Aura come and take my place in our bed!"

Then at last Cephalus realized the mistake that she had made. He began to tell her the truth, but the truth could not bring back her life. The little strength that remained to her fled away; she fell back in his arms; so long as she could look at anything, she looked into her husband's face and on his lips breathed out her life. It seemed to him that, before she died, her face changed and her expression became a happy one.

Arachne

ARACHNE was not famous for her birth or for her city, but only for her skill. Her father was a dyer of wool, her mother also was of no great family. She lived in a small village whose name is scarcely known. Yet her skill in weaving made her famous through all the great cities of Lydia. To see her wonderful work the nymphs of Tmolus would leave their vineyards, the nymphs of Pactolus would leave the golden waters of their river. It was a delight not only to see the cloth that she had woven, but to watch her at work, there was such beauty in the way she did it, whether she was winding the rough skeins into balls of wool, or smoothing it with her fingers, or drawing out the fleecy shiny wool into threads, or giving a twist to the spindle with her quick thumb, or putting in embroidery with her needle. You would think that she had learned the art from Minerva herself, the goddess of weaving.

Arachne, however, when people said this, would be offended at the idea of having had even so great a teacher as Minerva. "Let her come," she used to say, "and weave against me. If she won, she could do what she liked with me."

Minerva heard her words and put on the form of an old woman. She put false grey hair on her head, made her steps weak and tottering, and took a staff in her hand. Then she said to Arachne: "There are some advantages in old age. Long years bring experience. Do not, then, refuse my advice. Seek all the fame you like among men for your skill, but allow the goddess to take first place, and ask her forgiveness, you foolish girl, for the words which you have spoken. She will forgive you, if you ask her."

Archne dropped the threads from her hand and looked angrily at the old woman. She hardly kept her hands off her, and her face showed the anger that she felt. Then she spoke to the goddess in disguise: "Stupid old thing, what is wrong with you is that you have lived too long. Go and give advice to your daughters, if you have any. I am quite able to look after myself. As for what you say, why does not the goddess come here herself? Why does she avoid a contest with me?"

"She has come," Minerva replied, and she put off the old woman's disguise, revealing herself in her true form. The nymphs bowed down to worship her, and the women also who were there. Arachne alone showed no fear. Nevertheless she started, and a sudden blush came to her unwilling face and then faded away again, as the sky grows crimson at the moment of sunrise and then again grows pale. She persisted in what she had said already, and, stupidly longing for the desired victory, rushed headlong to her fate.

Minerva no longer refused the contest and gave no further advice. At once they both set up their looms and stretched out on them the delicate warp. The web was fastened to the beam; reeds separated the threads and through the threads went the sharp shuttles which their quick fingers sped. Quickly they worked, with their clothes tucked up round their breasts, their skilled hands moving backwards and forwards like lightning, not feeling the work since they were both so good at it. In their weaving they used all the colors that are made by the merchants of Tyre—purple of the oyster and every other dye, each shading into each, so that the eye could scarcely tell the difference between the finer shades, though the extreme colors were clear enough. So, after a storm of rain, when a rainbow spans the sky, between each color there is a great difference, but still between each an insensible shading. And in their work they wove in stiff threads of gold, telling ancient stories by pictures.

Minerva, in her weaving, showed the ancient citadel of Athens and the story of the old quarrel between her and Neptune, god of the sea, over the naming of this famous land. There you could see the twelve gods as witnesses, and there Neptune striking with his huge trident the barren rock from which leaped a stream of sea water. And there was Minerva herself, with shield and spear and helmet. As she struck the rock, there sprang up a green olive tree, and the victory was hers. Athens was her city, named from her other name, Athene.

As for Arachne, the pictures which she wove were of the deceitful loves of the gods. There was Europa, carried away by a bull over the sea. You would have thought it a real bull and real waves of water. Then she wove Jupiter coming to Danaë in a golden shower, to Aegina as a flame, to Mnemosyne, mother of the Muses, in the disguise of a shepherd. There was Neptune too, disguised as a dolphin, a horse or a ram. Every scene was different, and each scene had the surroundings that it ought to have. Round the edge of the web ran a narrow border filled with designs of flowers and sprays of ivy intertwined.

Neither Minerva nor Envy itself could find any fault with Arachne's work. Furious at the success of the mortal girl, Minerva tore to pieces the gorgeous web with its stories of the crimes of the gods. With the hard boxwood spindle that she held she struck Arachne on the head over and over again.

Arachne could not bear such treatment. In her injured pride she put a noose round her neck and hung herself. As she hung from the rope, Minerva, in pity, lifted her body and said: "You may keep your life, you rude and arrogant girl, but you and all your descendants will still hang."

Then, as she went out, she sprinkled over her some magic juices, and immediately her hair felt the poison it fell off; so did her nose and ears; her head became minute and all her body shrunk; her slender fingers were joined on to her body as legs; everything else was stomach, and now, turned into a spider, she still spins thread out of her own stomach and everywhere still exercises her old craft of weaving.

Niobe

NIOBE was the daughter of the great king Tantalus of Lydia. She married Amphion, the great singer and musician, to the sound of whose music the walls of Thebes had risen miraculously from the ground.

Before her marriage she had known Arachne, but she was not warned by Arachne's fate to give way to the gods and to speak reverently of them.

She had many reasons for being proud—the high birth of her husband and herself, their wealth, their royal power. But, proud as she was of all this, she was even prouder of her children. Indeed she might have been called the most happy of all mothers, if she had not thought herself so.

Once in Thebes the prophetess Manto, daughter of the old blind seer Tiresias, went through the streets, crying out: "Women of Thebes, go all together to Latona's temple. Bind your hair in wreaths of laurel and offer up prayers and incense to Latona and her two children, Apollo and Diana. The goddess is speaking to you through my mouth."

The women obeyed the prophetess, and went to the temple to pray, wearing their laurel wreaths; but they were interrupted on their way by Niobe, who came proudly walking, surrounded by a crowd of her friends, bright in her gold robes, and beautiful so far as anger allowed her to look beautiful, as she tossed back her fine head with the hair falling on her neck and shoulders. She stopped, and, looking haughtily around her, said: "What is the meaning of this madness? Will you give more honor to the gods, whom you have only heard of, than to those whom you have seen with your own eyes? Why should Latona have an altar and be worshiped, while I, just as divine as she is, have no incense burned to me? My father was Tantalus, the only mortal who has ever shared the meals of the gods. My mother is a sister of the Pleiades. One of my grandfathers is Atlas, who holds heaven on his shoulders; the other is Jupiter himself. The people of Asia fear me. I am Queen of Thebes, and the walls which rose to the music of my husband's lyre, together with all the people are under the rule of my husband and myself. In my house, wherever I turn my eyes, I see enormous riches. I am as beautiful as a goddess, and then, on top of all this, I have seven sons and seven daughters. Soon I shall have sons- and daughters-in-law.

"You see what reasons I have to be happy. How then can you prefer to me this Latona, whoever she may be? When she was about to give birth, there was no corner of the earth that would receive her. Only the little island of Delos, which floated on the surface of the sea, a wanderer as she was on land, took pity on her and allowed her to rest. Then she bore two children. I have seven times as many. I am happy. Who can deny it? And I shall remain happy. That also cannot be questioned. I have so much that I am safe. Even if Fortune took much from me, much more would be left. Even if I lost some of my children, I should still have many more than Latona's two. Indeed to have only two children is to be practically childless. Now leave this temple! You have sacrificed enough. Take off the wreaths from your hair!"

The Theban women obeyed her and left the sacrifice half finished. Still in their hearts they silently gave worship to the goddess.

Latona had heard the words of Niobe. In her heavenly place she spoke to her children, Apollo and Diana: "See how I, your mother, who am so proud of having given birth to you both, see how I am treated. People doubt whether I am a goddess at all, and, unless you help me, I shall no longer have altars at which I am worshiped. And this is not all. Niobe has added insult to injury. She has called me childless (let that fate be hers!) and has preferred her children to you."

At this Apollo interrupted her and said: "There is no need to say more. It would only delay their punishment." His sister Diana said the same. Swiftly they glided through the air and, with clouds enfolding them, alighted on the citadel of Cadmus's city, Thebes.

In front of the city there was a wide open plain, leveled out and hardened by the constant beat of horses' hooves and the rolling wheels of chariots. Here some of Amphion's seven sons were riding their strong horses, sitting on saddles that glowed bright with Tyrian purple and gripping in their hands reins that gleamed with gold. One of them, Ismenus, his mother's first born, was pulling hard on the foam-flecked bit as he made his horse turn a corner of the track, when suddenly he gave a cry and, with an arrow fixed in his heart, he dropped the reins and slowly slipped to the ground dead over the horse's right shoulder. Another brother, hearing through the empty air the sound of arrow that none can escape stuck quivering in his neck, at full speed. But, just as it was breaking into a gallop, the arrow that none can escape stuck quivering in his neck, with the iron point showing through at the other side. He pitched forward over the horse's mane and stained the ground with his warm blood. Two other brothers had finished their riding and were now enjoying a wrestling bout together. As they strained, breast to breast, each looking for a hold, one arrow pierced them both. Together they groaned, together their limbs relaxed as they fell to the ground, together they turned about them their dying eyes and breathed their last. Two more of Niobe's sons ran to lift up the dead bodies, but, while they were bending over them, they too felt the arrows in their backs and fell forward over the bodies which they had come to raise up. Now only the youngest brother was left. He stretched out his arms to Heaven and cried out: "O all you gods together, spare me, I pray you." He did not know that it was not necessary to pray to *all* the gods. Apollo pitied him, but it was too late. The shaft had already left the bow. The young man fell, pierced with only a light wound, but pierced to the heart.

News of the disaster came fast to the city, and Amphion, driven out of his mind by the loss of his fine sons, thrust a dagger into his heart, ending his sorrow and his life together.

Niobe, amazed that this could have happened and angry that the gods could have such power, came out of the city —a very different Niobe from the one who had turned the women away from Latona's altar and had strode through the streets, proud and envied by her friends. Now even her enemies might pity her. She threw herself down upon the cold bodies, crying and wildly kissing them. Then she lifted up her arms to Heaven and cried out: "Cruel Latona, feed your fierce heart on my sufferings! It is as if I myself had died seven times. Be happy in your hateful victory! And yet it is not a victory. In all my misery I still have more children than you in your happiness. Even after all these deaths, I am still the winner."

As she spoke there came the ringing sound of a taut bowstring, a sound that terrified everyone except Niobe herself. Suffering had made her bold.

In front of their brothers' bodies their sisters were standing, in black robes and with loose hair. One of these was just pulling from the wound the arrow that stuck there, when she sank forward, dead, over the body that she was tending. A second sister, while she was trying to console her mother in her grief, suddenly stopped speaking, doubled-up by an unseen wound. Others died as they turned to run away, and one was killed standing speechless and motionless in fear. Now six had perished, and only the youngest one remained. Her mother threw her arms about her, covering and hiding her in her dress. "Oh leave me just one," she cried, "my youngest one. Out of many I only ask now for one, and that one the smallest."

Even while she spoke, the child for whose life she was begging fell dead. Deprived of everything, the poor mother sat down among the lifeless bodies of her sons, her daughters, her husband. Sorrow made her stiff as stone. The breeze did not stir the hair around her forehead; her face was white and bloodless; her eyes stood fixed like stones in her sad cheeks; there was nothing of her that seemed alive; her very tongue froze to the roof of her mouth; the blood ceased to run in her veins; her neck could no longer bend, nor could she move her arms and her feet. All her flesh and all the inside of her body became hard rock. Still her tears flowed. Soon came a great rushing wind which whirled her away and carried her to her own country, setting her down on the top of a mountain. Here she still weeps and to this day the tears well out from the marble.

Acis and Galatea

ON the rocky coast of Sicily once lived the giant
Cyclops, called Polyphemus. He was the son of
Neptune, but he despised both gods and men. In the middle of his forehead was set one great eye, an eye which,
later on, he was destined to lose at the hands of the Greek
hero Ulysses on his return from Troy. His mind was rough
and churlish as was his great hairy body. Indeed it was no
pleasure to look at him or to be near him.

Once, as he wandered along the shore, supporting his
heavy steps on a huge staff as tall as the mast of a ship,
and feeding his flocks of sheep, he caught sight of the sea
nymph Galatea, and immediately, so far as anything so
uncouth could feel love, he fell in love with her. She, however, loved the young shepherd Acis, and he returned her
love, keeping himself for her alone.

As for the Cyclops, Galatea hated him and his wooing
almost as much as she loved her Acis. Yet this did not
make the Cyclops give up his attempts to win her heart.
He forgot his flocks and his caves, with their stores of

cheeses and of milk. Now he began to think of his appearance, and of how he could become charming. He combed his shaggy hair with a rake, and cut off his stiff beard with a sickle. Then he would look at his rough face in a pool of water, and try to make the expression more pleasing.

There was a high promontory which, shaped like a wedge, jutted out into the sea, with water on either side of it. Here the savage Cyclops climbed up and sat down. His woolly sheep followed him at random, since he paid no attention to them. In front of his feet he threw down his great staff, and took out his pipe, which was made of a hundred reeds. The mountains all around felt the sound of his piping, and Galatea herself, who, in the shelter of a rock a long way away was resting in the arms of Acis, heard clearly the words that the Cyclops sang.

"O Galatea," he sang, "you who are whiter than the leaves of the snowy privet, more like a flower than all the flowery meadows, standing straight and tall as the elder tree, brighter than crystal, gay and playful as a young kid, smoother than shells polished by the rolling waves, more lovely than the sun in winter or the shade in summer, more glorious than apples, more to be admired than the tall plane tree, shining more brightly than ice, sweeter than the ripe grape, softer than swan's down or curdled milk, O, and if only you would not run away from me, more beautiful than a fresh green garden! And yet, Galatea, you are more headstrong than an untamed heifer, harder than old oak wood, falser than water, tougher than willow twigs, less to be moved than these rocks, more violent than a river torrent, vainer than the peacock when it is praised, fiercer than fire, sharper than thorns, more surly than a she-bear with young, deafer than sea water, more relentless than a snake that is trodden on, and (this particularly I would like you not to be) more fleet of foot not only than a stag before the hounds but even than the winds and the flying breezes.

"If only you knew me well you would wish that you had not fled from me. I have a whole mountainside to live in, deep caves where the sun's heat never comes in summer, nor does the cold in winter. In my orchard the boughs are weighed down with apples. On my vines grow grapes as yellow as gold, and purple grapes as well. Both kinds are meant for you. You with your own hands will be able to pick in the shady woods the wild strawberries, cherries in the autumn, and plums, not only the juicy black kind, but also the big yellow ones that look like wax. If you marry me, you can have chestnuts as well, and all the trees will be your servants. Then there are my flocks, so many that I do not bother to count them, my goats and my kids, and always plenty of snow-white milk.

"And if you want a pet to play with, I should not give you anything ordinary and common like a fawn, or a hare or a kid, a pair of doves or a nest of birds taken from a rock. No, I have got two bear cubs for you to play with, so like each other that you could not tell them apart. When I found them I said: 'I'll keep these for the girl I love.'

"O come now, Galatea! Raise your bright head from the blue sea, and do not despise what I offer you! I have a good idea of myself now, since I recently looked at my face in the mirror of a clear pool. I liked what I saw. Look

how big I am! A great mass of hair juts out over my fore-head and falls over my shoulders like a forest. You must not think it ugly to be covered all over the body, as I am, with thick shaggy hair. Trees are ugly without their leaves, and sheep without their wool. Men, too, ought to be cov-ered in bristling hair like mine. It is true that I have only one eye in the middle of my forehead, but this eye is as big as a cartwheel.

"O Galatea, I fear none of the gods, but I fear you and your anger. It would be easier to bear your refusal of me, if you refused everyone else. How is it that you can love Acis and prefer him to me? I wish I could get near him. He'd soon find out what strength there is in me. I'd tear his heart out of his body, I'd pull him to pieces, limb from limb, and scatter the pieces over the fields and over the waters of your sea. For I am on fire with love, and all the more on fire because I am rejected. It seems as though I have a volcano in my heart, and you, Galatea, do not mind at all."

So the Cyclops sang and roared over the sea. Then he got to his feet to wander restlessly about, just as a bull, furious when the cow is taken from him, cannot stand still but paces through the woods and well-known pastures.

Suddenly he saw Galatea and Acis hiding under the rock in each other's arms. "I see you," he shouted out, "and I will make sure that this meeting of yours will be your last."

His huge terrible cries made the whole of Etna ring and re-echo with the sound. Galatea, in terror, sprang back into the sea and dived beneath the waves. Acis turned to run, but the Cyclops ran after him, tore a great piece from a mountain side and hurled it at the young man. Only the corner of the huge mass reached him, but it was enough to bury him entirely beneath earth and rock.

The gods had pity on Acis. Through the earth beneath which he was buried, first crimson blood began to ooze up; then, after a little time, the red color began to fade away; now the color was like muddy river water, swollen by a storm; then the great mass of rock cracked open, and a tall green reed shot up through the crack. Next, through the opening came a stream of bright leaping water, a new fresh river, and, standing waist-high in the stream, appeared the god of the river, a beautiful youth, with small fresh-grown horns all wreathed with shining reeds upon his forehead. This was Acis, just as he had been except for the horns and except that he was bigger. The river joined its waters with the sea and was called after its own god.

Glaucus and Scylla

G LAUCUS, a god of the sea, was once a mortal man. He lived in the island of Euboea, and even then, in his mortal life, he was devoted to the sea, and spent all his time upon it, sometimes dragging in his nets full of fish, sometimes sitting on the rocks with rod and line, looking out over the blue water to the mountains and the islands.

There is a part of the shore where green grass runs down to the water. Here no horned cattle have ever grazed, nor have peaceful sheep cropped the grass, nor hairy goats. No busy bees have ever crossed the meadow in search of honey, nor have human hands plucked the flowers for garlands. It is a deserted place, and Glaucus was the first ever to sit down on the soft turf, where he spread out his lines and wet nets to dry, and began to count the fish that he had caught, laying them all out upon the grass in rows.

While he was doing so, he was amazed to see that the fish, as soon as they were laid on the grass, began to stir and to wriggle; then they began to move about on land as though they were on water, and soon they all moved down again to the sea and swam away.

Glaucus stood for a long time in amazement, wondering what could be the reason for this strange happening. Was it one of the gods who had given this power to the fish? Or was it the effect of some magic in the grass? He decided to see whether the grass would have any effect on him and, taking up a handful of grass and flowers together, began to eat it. Hardly had he begun to taste the strange juices when he felt his heart trembling and longing for an entirely different way of life. "Farewell, Earth!" he cried out. "I shall never come back to you again." And he plunged into the sea.

The gods of the sea welcomed him and made him one of them. They purged away from him everything that was mortal, first by repeating over him nine times a magic charm, then by washing his body in the streams of a hundred rivers. As the rivers poured their waters over his head, Glaucus lost consciousness. When his senses came back to him, he found that both his body and his mind had changed. Now he had a long streaming beard, dark green hair that floated beside him in the waves, huge shoulders, sea-blue arms and curved legs that ended in the fins of fishes. Blowing on a horn made of a deep-sea shell, he swam and dived with the Nereids and other gods and goddesses of the ocean.

There was a mortal girl, Scylla, who, in her pride, had refused all offers of marriage, and who used to come and talk with the nymphs of the sea. Glaucus fell in love with her and told her his story, wishing to show her that, though he was a god, he was also able to understand mortals. She, however, fled from him, as she had fled from everybody else, and Glaucus, angry and bitter at being refused, went for help to the wonderful palace and island of the goddess Circe.

With his huge arms and sinuous legs and tail he swam past Sicily and Italy and came to the grassy hills and woods where Circe had her palace. In the woods were bears and lions, panthers, tigers, beasts of all kinds—all once men, but now turned into these shapes by Circe's enchantments. Circe welcomed him and he said to her: "O goddess, have pity upon a god. You alone, if you think me worthy of your help, can help me in my love. I myself know the power of magic herbs, since it was by them that I became a god. Now I am in love with a mortal. Her name is Scylla and she lives on the coast of Italy, opposite Sicily. I beg you to use some charm or some magic herb to help me. I do not want you to cure me of my love, but to make her love me with at least a little of the feeling that I have for her."

Circe, however, was a goddess whose heart was very easily moved to the love either of gods or of men. When she saw Glaucus, she desired to have him for herself and said to him: "It would be much better to leave someone who does not want you and to follow someone who does. You who might be wooed yourself ought not to waste your time in wooing. And to give you confidence in your own charm I tell you that I myself, the daughter of the sun, a goddess, would like to be your love."

To this Glaucus replied: "I can tell you that, so long as

Scylla is alive, leaves will grow in the sea and seaweed on the tops of the mountains before my love changes."

Circe was angry. She could not hurt him, and perhaps since she loved him, she did not want to. All her anger turned against the woman who had been preferred to her. At once she mixed together the juices of terrible herbs and, as she did so, she muttered charms that are used by Hecate, the goddess of witches. Then she put on a blue cloak and went out through the wild beasts that licked her hands and fawned upon her as she passed. She walked over the waves of the sea as though it was dry land, just skimming the surface with dry feet, and she came to the channel where Italy looks across at Sicily.

There was a little rock pool shaped like a crescent moon, a place where Scylla loved to come and rest. Here she used to refresh herself in the heat of midday, and in this pool, before Scylla arrived, Circe put the terrible poisons which she had brought, again murmuring over them her charmed words.

Then Scylla came and had gone into the pool as far as her waist when, looking downwards, she saw all round the lower part of her body the shapes of barking monsters. When first she saw them she could not believe that they were actually parts of her body, but fled away terrified at the sight of the fierce dog's heads. As she fled, however, she drew with her what she was running away from. Putting down her hand to feel the flesh of her thighs, her legs and her feet, all she felt was the gaping heads of dogs, fearful as Cerberus himself. Instead of feet she stood on the hairy necks and savage faces of wild beasts.

Glaucus, who loved her, wept for her and fled far away from Circe who had used her charms so cruelly. As for Scylla, she remained fixed to the rock in that place. Opposite her was the fig tree and great whirlpool of Charybdis. Later, when she had a chance, she tried to revenge herself on Circe by destroying the sailors of Ulysses, who had been Circe's friend.

Bellerophon

B ELLEROPHON was son of the King of Corinth and grew up to be a young man of remarkable strength and beauty, brave also, and ready to undertake any difficult adventure.

Soon after he grew to manhood he unluckily and by accident killed one of his relations and, to avoid the guilt of blood, he left his native land and went to live in Argos.

Here Proetus was king and here Bellerophon received a generous welcome. The king admired the young man's courage and beauty; he was glad to have his services in peace and war, and raised him to a position of honor in his court. Bellerophon might have lived for long in Argos, had it not been that the king's wife Antea fell in love with him. She approached him with endearing words, begging him to take her from her husband. Bellerophon, grateful to the king for his hospitality and for his many kindnesses, indignantly refused to listen to the shameful suggestions of Antea. Then her love turned to hatred. She went to Proetus and said: "If you have any respect for your wife, I demand that this young man be put to death. He is on fire with love for me, and has already attempted by force to take me away from you."

Proetus believed the false words of his wife, but still he did not wish himself to have the guilt and unpopularity of putting the young man to death. He therefore sent him to visit his father-in-law Iobates, King of Lycia in Asia Minor, and before he left he gave him a sealed message in which was written: "If you love me and value my friendship, ask no questions but immediately put the bearer of this message to death."

Bellerophon took the message with no suspicion that he was carrying his own death-warrant, and set out on his voyage across the sea to Lycia. When he arrived King Iobates, knowing him to be the favorite of the King of Argos, welcomed him warmly and feasted him in the rich halls of his palace. They were merry and friendly together at the feast, but when it was over Bellerophon gave the King the message which he had brought, and the King read it in sorrow and amazement, unwilling to believe that so gallant a young man could have injured his protector, unwilling too to offend against the sacred laws of hospitality by killing a stranger whom he had entertained in his own halls. Nevertheless he could not refuse to obey the clear instructions of the King of Argos. A plan occurred to him by which it seemed certain that the young man would meet his death, while the king himself would not incur the guilt of having directly brought it about. Bellerophon had already offered to help the king in any way in which his services could be used. Now the king ordered him to find and to destroy the Chimera, an invincible monster that lived in rocky caves and ravaged all the country around. The Chimera had a lion's head, the body of a great shaggy she-goat, and a dragon's tail. Out of its mouth it breathed such blasts of fire and smoke that no one could approach it. It moved with incredible speed, hunting down men and cattle, so that for miles around its rocky lair the country was a wilderness.

Bellerophon knew the difficulties and dangers of his task, but he gladly and willingly undertook it. His courage, however, would not have proved enough if he had not been helped by the goddess Minerva. She told him that he could never conquer the Chimera without the help of Pegasus, the winged horse who had sprung to life from the blood of Medusa, whom Perseus slew, and who now lived on Mount Helicon with the Muses, never yet having felt the weight of a man upon his back. So Bellerophon set out once more on a long journey. He found the horse, a wonderful and swift animal, snow-white and smooth as silk not only over all his skin but also where the gleaming feathery wings lay along his shoulders. For a whole day Bellerophon tried to throw a bridle round the animal's neck, but Pegasus would never allow him to come close enough to do so. Whenever Bellerophon approached, the horse would either gallop away out of reach or would rise on wings in the air, alighting further off in the cool meadows where he grazed. In the evening, worn out and despairing, Bellerophon lay down to sleep. He dreamed that Minerva had come to him and given him a golden bridle. On waking up he found that this was actually what had happened. At his side was a beautiful bridle of gold and, with this in his hand, he immediately set out again to look for Pegasus. When the horse saw the bridle, he bowed his head and came gently forward, willingly allowing Bellerophon to bridle and to mount him. Then he sprang into the air and sped like a shooting star through the clouds to the country where the Chimera lived; for the horse was a divine horse, knowing exactly for what reason he was wanted.

Flying over the deep gullies and rocky caves in the mountains, Bellerophon saw beneath him the red glow of fire and smoke ascending into the air. He checked the course of Pegasus and flew nearer to the earth, and soon appeared the vast body of the monster as it came raging out of its lair. Pegasus hovered over it as a hawk hovers above its prey, and first Bellerophon shot his arrows into the great goat-like body below him, until the ground was drenched in blood. Then he swooped down through the clouds of smoke, thrusting his sword over and over again into the animal's neck and flanks. It was not long before the Chimera lay dead and sprawling on the ground. Then Bellerophon cut off its head and said good-bye to the noble horse who had helped him, since Minerva had told him that once his task was accomplished, he must let the animal go. Pegasus was never again mounted by any mortal man. He sped away like lightning. Some say that he went back to the grassy pastures of Helicon and that where his hoof struck the ground there issued forth the fountain of Hippocrene. Others say that it was at this time that Jupiter set the winged horse among the stars.

Bellcrophon himself returned to King Iobates carrying

with him the head of the Chimera. The king was glad that the monster had been destroyed and he admired the courage of the young man who had destroyed it. Still he felt bound to carry out the instructions of the King of Argos and secure Bellerophon's death. Next he sent him to fight against the Solymi, a tribe of fierce mountaineers who lived upon the borders of Lycia and who had conquered the king's armies whenever they had been sent against them. Bellerophon, with a small force, marched into the mountains, killed or made prisoners of the whole tribe, and returned without a wound.

Next he was sent against the warrior nation of the Amazons, the fierce women who had conquered so many armies of men in battle. These also Bellerophon defeated, and now the king determined on a last plan by which he could do the will of the King of Argos. He picked out of his forces the best and strongest of his fighting men, and told them to lay an ambush for Bellerophon as he was on his way back from his conquest of the Amazons. Again the gods preserved him. With his own hand he killed every one of his attackers, and when he reached the king's court Iobates exclaimed: "There can be no doubt that the young man is innocent. Otherwise the gods would not have saved his life so often."

He gave Bellerophon his daughter to be his wife, sharing with him his riches and his throne. And when Iobates died, Bellerophon became King of Lycia.

Midas

OLD Silenus, the fat companion of the god Bacchus, was nearly always drunk. Once in the country of Phrygia, when he was lying on the ground drowsy with wine, some countrymen found him. They bound him in wreaths of flowers and took him to their king, who was called Midas.

Midas reverenced both Bacchus and his followers. He was glad to see old Silenus and entertained him hospitably. For ten days and nights he feasted him and on the eleventh day joyfully brought him back to Bacchus.

So pleased was Bacchus to find his companion safe and sound that he said to Midas: "Choose anything you like for a gift, and it shall be given to you."

Midas made bad use of the opportunity which the god had given him. "What I should like," he said, "is that everything which I touch should be turned to gold."

Bacchus granted his prayer, but wished that he had made a better choice, since what he had asked for would only bring him sorrow. But Midas went away full of joy and at once decided to try the effects of his new power. Hardly daring to believe in it, he broke off a twig from a small oak tree. Immediately the twig turned to gold. He picked up a stone from the ground, and the stone sparkled and shone with precious metal. He touched a clod of earth, and the clod became a great nugget of gold. He let his hand stray over the ears of growing corn, and the harvest was a harvest of gold. He picked an apple from a tree and, when he held it in his hand, it was like one of the apples of the Hesperides. If he touched the pillars in his palace, the pillars gleamed and shone. When he washed his hands, the running water that he poured over them turned to a golden shower. As he thought of turning everything to gold, it seemed to him that he was happy beyond his wildest dreams.

Then, as he was still rejoicing in his new power, his servants brought out a table covered with fine meats and bread. But when he put out his hand to take the bread, it immediately became hard and stiff. When he put a piece of meat in his mouth and started to bite it, he found that his teeth were biting on hard metal. He mixed water with his wine to drink, but, when he raised the glass to his lips, it was molten metal that flowed into his mouth.

This was far from being what he had expected. He was rich indeed, but also most miserable. Now he longed to escape from his wealth, and hated the very thing for which he had prayed. All the food in the world could not relieve his hunger. His throat was parched with thirst. He was tortured by the hateful gold. Lifting up to the sky his shining arms and hands, he prayed: "O Father Bacchus, forgive me my mistake! Have pity on me, and take away this gift that seemed so very different from what it really is!"

The gods are kind. Midas had confessed his fault and Bacchus made him as he had been before. "And," he said, "so that you may not remain with your skin all covered in the gold which you stupidly desired, go to the river Pactolus that flows past the great city of Sardis. Follow the stream through the mountains till you come to its source. There, where the foaming river comes gushing from the rocks, bathe your head and body. This, at the same time, will wash away your sin."

Midas did as the god had told him. The golden touch passed from his body into the water. Even to this day the river rolls over golden sands and carries gold dust to the sea.

Now Midas had had enough of wealth. He wandered through the fields and forests, worshiping the goat god Pan, who lives in the caves of the mountains. His mind, however, was still dull and foolish, and soon once more did him harm.

Near the city of Sardis stands the great mountain Tmolus, and here one day Pan was singing his songs to the beautiful nymphs and playing to them on his pipe made of reeds joined together with wax. As he sang he dared to say that his own music was better than Apollo's, and challenged the god of music himself to a contest with Tmolus as a judge.

Apollo came, and Tmolus, god of the mountain, took his seat, shaking the trees away from the sides of his head. Round his dark hair was a wreath of oak, and acorns hung about his hollow temples. He looked at Pan, the god of shepherds, and said: "See, the judge has not been slow. He is ready to listen."

Then Pan made his music on his country pipes. It was rough music, but it charmed Midas, who happened to be among the listeners. When Pan had finished, Tmolus turned his face towards Apollo and, as he turned, the forests turned with him.

On his golden hair the god wore a wreath of laurel from Mount Parnassus. His long cloak, sweeping the ground, was dyed red with Tyrian dyes. In his left hand he held his lyre, bright with ivory and precious stones. In his right hand he held the plectrum to pluck the strings. Even from the way he stood you could tell that he was a musician. Then he plucked the strings, and soon Tmolus, charmed utterly by that sweet and noble music, told Pan that his pipes were no match for the lyre of Apollo.

All agreed with the judgment of the mountain god— all except Midas, who kept disputing it and calling it unjust. Apollo then decided that he was unworthy to have human ears. He made them grow long, filled them with rough grey hair, and made them able to move from the base. In all other ways Midas was human: only as a punishment for his bad taste, he had the ears of an ass.

Naturally he was ashamed of them and covered them up in a purple turban which he wore upon his head. But the servant who used to cut his hair discovered his secret. He dared not tell others what he had discovered, but he could not bear to keep the secret to himself. So he went out and dug a hole in the ground. Kneeling down he

whispered into the hole: "King Midas has asses' ears."
Then he carefully put back the earth and went away, re-
lieved that he had spoken the words, even though no
one had heard them. But a crop of whispering reeds
sprang up in the place, and, when they were full-grown
and swayed by the winds of the autumn, they repeated
the words that were buried at their roots. "Midas has asses'
ears," they said to every breeze, and the breezes carried
on the news.

Atalanta's Race

THE huntress Atalanta, whom Meleager, before he died, had loved, could run faster even than the fastest runners among men. Nor was her beauty inferior to her swiftness of foot; both were beyond praise.

When Atalanta asked the oracle about whom she ought to marry, the god replied: "Do not take a husband, Atalanta. If you do, it will bring disaster on you. Yet you will not escape, and though you will continue to live, you will not be yourself."

Terrified by these words, Atalanta lived in the dark woods unmarried. There were many men who wished to marry her, but to them, in their eagerness, she said: "No one can have me for his wife unless first he beats me in a race. If you will, you may run with me. If any of you wins, he shall have me as a prize. But those who are defeated will have death for their reward. These are the conditions for the race."

Cruel indeed she was, but her beauty had such power that numbers of young men were impatient to race with her on these terms.

There was a young man called Hippomenes, who had come to watch the contest. At first he had said to himself: "What man in his senses would run such a risk to get a wife?" and he had condemned the young men for being too madly in love. But when he saw her face and her body all stripped for the race—a face and a body like Venus's own—he was lost in astonishment and, stretching out his hands, he said: "I had no right to blame the young men. I did not know what the prize was for which they were running."

As he spoke his own heart caught on fire with love for her and, in jealous fear, he hoped that none of the young men would be able to beat her in the race. Then he said to himself: "But why should not I try my fortune? When one takes a risk, the gods help one."

By now the race had started, and the girl sped past him on feet that seemed to have wings. Though she went fast as an arrow, he admired her beauty still more. Indeed she looked particularly beautiful when running. In the breeze her hair streamed back over her ivory shoulders; the ribbons with their bright borders fluttered at her knees; the white of her young body flushed rose-red, as when a purple awning is drawn over white marble and makes the stone glow with its own color. While Hippomenes fixed his eyes on her, she reached the winning post and was crowned with the victor's garland. The young men, with groans, suffered the penalty of death according to the agreement which they had made.

Their fate, however, had no effect on Hippomenes. He came forward and, fixing his eyes on Atalanta, said: "Why do you win an easy glory by conquering these slow movers? Now run with me. If I win, it will be no disgrace to you. I am a king's son and Neptune is my great-grandfather. And, if you defeat me, it will be an honor to be able to say that you defeated Hippomenes."

As he spoke, Atalanta looked at him with a softer expression in her eyes. She wondered whether she really wanted to conquer or to be conquered. She thought to herself: "What god, envious of beautiful young men, wants to destroy this one and makes him seek marriage with me at the risk of his dear life? In my opinion, I am not worth it. It is not his beauty that touches me (though I might easily be touched by that); it is because he is still only a boy. And then there is his courage, and the fact that he is willing to risk so much for me. Why should he die, simply because he wants to live with me? I wish he would go, while he still may, and realize that it is fatal to want to marry me. Indeed he deserves to live. If only I were happier, if only the fates had not forbidden me to marry, he would be the man that I would choose."

Meanwhile Atalanta's father and the whole people demanded that the race should take place. Hippomenes prayed to Venus and said: "O goddess, you put this love into my heart. Now be near me in my trial and aid me!"

A gentle breeze carried his prayer to the goddess and she was moved by it. Little time, however, remained in which she could help him. But it happened that she had just returned from her sacred island of Cyprus, where in one of her temple gardens grows a golden apple tree. The leaves are gold; the branches and the fruit rattle with metal as the wind stirs them. Venus had in her hand three golden apples which she had just picked from this tree. Now she came down to earth, making herself visible only to Hippomenes, and showed him how to use the apples.

Then the trumpets sounded and the two runners darted forward from the starting post, skimming over the sandy course with feet so light that it would seem they might have run over the sea or over the waving heads of standing corn. The crowd shouted their applause. "Now, Hippomenes," they cried, "run as you have never run before! You are winning." It would be difficult to say whether Hippomenes or Atalanta herself was most pleased with this encouragement. For some time Atalanta, though she might have passed the young man, did not do so. She ran by his side, looking into his face. Then, half unwillingly, she left him behind. He, with parched throat and straining lungs, followed after; still the winning post was far in the distance; and now he took one of the golden apples which Venus had given him and threw it in her way. The girl looked with wonder at the shining fruit and, longing to have it, stopped running so that she could pick it up. Hippomenes passed her and again the spectators shouted out their applause. Soon, however, Atalanta made up the ground that she had lost and again left Hippomenes behind. He threw the second apple, once more took the lead and once more was overtaken. Now they were in sight of the winning post, and Hippomenes, with a prayer to Venus, threw the last apple rather sideways, so that it went some distance from the course. Atalanta seemed to hesitate whether she should go after it or not, but Venus made her go, and, when she had picked up the apple, she made it heavier, handicapping the girl not only by the time she had lost but by the weight of what she was carrying. This time she could not catch up Hippomenes. He passed the winning post first and claimed her as his bride.

Then, indeed, Hippomenes should have offered thanks to Venus, but he forgot entirely the goddess who had helped him, neither giving thanks nor making sacrifice.

Venus was angry and determined to make an example of them both. On their way to the home of Hippomenes they came to a holy temple, sacred to the mother of the gods, great Cybele. No mortal was allowed to pass the night in this temple, so hallowed was the spot; but Venus put it into the hearts of Hippomenes and Atalanta, who were tired from their journey, to rest there all night and treat the temple of the goddess as though it were a common inn. So in the most holy of the temple's shrines, where wooden images of the ancient gods turned away their eyes in horror at the profanation, they rested together. But the terrible goddess, her head crowned with a crown of towers, appeared to them. She covered their necks, which had been so smooth, with tawny manes of hair; their fingers became sharp claws, and their arms turned to legs. Most of their weight went to their chests, and behind them they swept the sandy ground with long tails. Instead of the palace they had hoped for, they lived in the savage woods, a lion and a lioness, terrible to others but, when Cybele needed them, tame enough to draw her chariot, champing the iron bits between their gnashing jaws.

Ceyx and Halcyone

CEYX was the son of Lucifer, the morning star. Halcyone, his wife, was the daughter of Aeolus, god of the winds. The gods who were their parents could not save them from disaster; but in the end they were happy.

Once Ceyx, disturbed by many strange events which had taken place in his kingdom, decided to go on a voyage across the sea to consult a famous oracle. He told his faithful wife Halcyone what he intended to do, and when he told her, her face became as pale as boxwood, tears ran down her cheeks and she felt cold to the marrow of her bones. "What have I done, dearest husband," she said, "to make you change? Why have you stopped caring for me above everything? Can you go away with an easy mind and leave your Halcyone behind you? If your journey was by land, though I should be sad, I should not be frightened. But the sea and the stern face of the waters terrify me. Only the other day I saw some broken planks tossed up on the shore; and I have often read men's names on empty tombs. Do not be rash just because my father keeps the winds in their prison. Once the winds are let out and reach the open sea, nothing can be done to stop them. I have seen them when I was a little girl in my father's house, and I know what they are like. But if nothing that I can say can make you change your mind, if you are so fixed on going, then, dear husband, take me with you too. Then at least we shall face the storms together and I shall have nothing to fear except what I can see and feel."

Ceyx, who loved his wife as much as she loved him, was moved by her words and her tears. But he did not want to put off his journey, nor did he wish her to share the dangers of it. Many arguments he used in trying to comfort her timid heart, but still he did not convince her. The only thing that consoled her at all was when he said: "I know this separation will seem long to both of us, but I swear to you by the fire of my father's star, that, unless the fates prevent me, I will return before two moons have passed."

This promise of return made her rather happier, and Ceyx immediately ordered his ship to be made ready for the sea. When she saw it, Halcyone, as though she could read the future, began to tremble and the tears came again to her eyes. When she had kissed her husband and said good-bye, she fainted. Ceyx himself tried to think of some excuse for delaying, but already the rowers, sitting in order at their benches, were pulling back the oars to their strong breasts, churning the sea white beneath their regular strokes. Then Halcyone opened her eyes, still wet with tears. She saw her husband standing on the high stern and waving his hand to her. She waved back to him, and, as the

ship went further from the land and she could no longer
see his face, she still followed the fast-moving ship with her
eyes. When the ship had disappeared, she fixed her gaze
on the sails that bellied out at the top of the mast. Then she
went to her room and threw herself down upon her bed.
Her room and her bed made her cry again, since they re-
minded her that a part of herself had gone away.

Meanwhile the ship had left the harbor and a fresh
breeze began to sing in the ropes. The captain shipped the
oars, and spread all sail. So all day she ran over the sea, but
at nightfall, when the land on either side was far away, the
waves began to whiten and the wind began to blow more
strongly. "Quick!" shouted the captain, "lower the yard,
and reef the sails." The wind blowing in his face took away
the sound of his words, still, of their own accord, the sailors began to draw in the oars, to close the oar holes and to
reef the sails. Some bailed out water, others hurriedly
made their different preparations to face the storm. And
now every moment the storm increased in force. The fierce
winds came rushing from every direction, lashing up the
angry waves. The captain himself stood in terror, admit-
ting that he did not know what orders to give, since the
weight and mass of wind and water were too powerful for
his skill. All was in an uproar—men shouting, squalls hissing through the rigging, the waves roaring and thunder
crashing out through the upper air. Waves, running
mountain-high, seemed to be combing the lowering clouds
with the spray that they swept with them. In their troughs
you could see the yellow sand, churned up from the bottom of the sea.

As for the ship, sometimes it was lifted high up in the air so that the terrified sailors could look down into the gulfs beneath; sometimes it was plunged downwards as though to the depths of hell, and from the depth they looked up to heaven towering above them. Waves battered and thudded on the ship's sides, like iron battering rams on the wall of a besieged city. Soon the wedges that tightened the hull began to work loose. More and more of the sea came in, and meanwhile sheets of rain fell from the bursting clouds. It seemed as though the whole of heaven was pouring itself into the sea, while the swelling sea was itself mounting into the sky. No stars were to be seen. Everything was black night, except when the fitful lightning flashed along the clouds and made the waves gleam red.

As when soldiers are storming a city's wall and, when one or two have found a foothold, the task becomes easier for the others, so when one wave had leaped over the ship's side, others followed and soon the ship was half full of water. Skill and courage had failed. Some of the sailors were weeping, others stood dumb with terror; some prayed for at least burial ashore, others thought of their brothers, their wives or their children whom they had left behind.

Ceyx thought of Halcyone and only her name was upon his lips. He longed only for her, but he was glad that she was not with him. He would have liked to turn his eyes for the last time towards his own country and towards his home, but he had no idea in which direction they lay.

A whirlwind snapped off the mast; the rudder too was

smashed. Then one last wave, as though proud in victory, curled itself up above the others, and with a roaring crash fell headlong on the ship, crushing the deck and sending it to the very bottom of the sea. Most of the men were dragged down with her and died, sucked in by the whirlpool where she sank. Some still clung to bits of wreckage, and among them was Ceyx, whose hands were used to holding a scepter.

As he struggled to keep himself afloat, he called in vain on his father Lucifer, and on his father-in-law, the king of the winds. But chiefly, as he swam, the name of Halcyone was on his lips. It was she whom he most remembered, and he prayed that the waves might carry his body back to her so that her dear hands might prepare him for burial. So long as he had strength to swim, and so long as the waves allowed him to open his mouth, he spoke her name and murmured it to the waters that were closing over him. A black and curving wave broke over his head, plunging him down beneath the whitening rush of foam. At dawn Lucifer, the morning star, was dim and hard to see. He could not leave his place in heaven, but he wrapped up his light in thick clouds.

Halcyone meanwhile, knowing nothing of what had happened, was counting up the nights that would have to pass before her husband returned; she was busy weaving clothes for him to wear when he came back, and imagining an arrival which would never take place. She was careful to burn incense to all the gods, and especially to Juno, constantly praying for her husband, who no longer existed. She prayed that he might be safe, that he might come back, and that he should never love anyone more than her. This last was the only one of the prayers that could be granted.

Juno could not bear to listen to prayers that concerned one who was already dead. She spoke to her messenger Iris, the goddess of the rainbow. "Iris," she said, "my faithful servant, go to the drowsy court of Sleep, and order him to send to Halcyone a dream in the shape of dead Ceyx to tell her the truth of what has happened."

Iris then put on her thousand-colored veil, and, marking the sky as she went in the great curve of a rainbow, came to the hidden cloudy dwelling of the King of Sleep.

Near the land of the Cimmerians, in a hollow mountain, there is a deep long cave, the home and secret hiding place of heavy Sleep. Neither rising, nor setting, nor at midday can the sun dart his rays into this place. A cloud of mist and dark twilight shadows are like a breath coming up from the ground. Here no crested cock watches for the dawn and crows, no dogs bark to break the silence, nor geese, still more to be relied upon than dogs. There is no sound of wild beasts, or cattle, or branches moving in the breeze or noisy talk of men. It is the home of utter silence, though from the end of the cave there flows the stream of Lethe, river of forgetfulness, whose sliding waves, gently stirring the pebbles over which they run, invite to sleep. In front of the cave's entrance there grows a mass of poppies, and there are all the numberless herbs whose drowsy juices Night gathers and spreads over the darkening earth. The house has no door, lest there should be hinges to creak; nor does any servant keep watch on the threshold. But in the middle of the cave there is a couch of ebony

raised above the floor. The couch is as soft as down, black in color and covered with dark coverlets, and on it lies the god Sleep, with his limbs stretched out in weariness. Around him lie the shapes of empty dreams, able to imitate every form of life, innumerable as are the grains of corn in harvest, the leaves of the forest, or the sand lying on the shore.

When Iris had entered this cave and brushed away with her hands the dreams that clustered round her, the sacred place was lit up with the shining of her garments. The god could hardly lift his heavy eyelids and again and again slipped back into sleep as he tried to raise his chin from his breast. Finally he roused himself, propped himself on an elbow and asked her (for he recognized her) why she had come.

"Sweet Sleep," she said, "you who bring peace to everything, most mild of all the gods, you who ease the heart and are the refuge from care, you who calm our tired bodies and make them fit for work again—I ask you to shape a dream in the form of King Ceyx and send it to his wife Halcyone, to tell her the story of his shipwreck. This is what Juno commands."

Iris then went away, for she already felt stealing over her the drowsiness of sleep. She went back on the curve of the rainbow by which she had come.

The god chose out one of his sons, Morpheus, to do the task which had been given him. He told him what he must do, then once more let his body relax in idleness upon the high couch.

Morpheus on his soft and noiseless wings flew through the darkness to the city where Halcyone was queen. Then he put off his wings and took on the shape of Ceyx, but with a pale worn face like that of a dead man. So he stood naked by the bed of the unhappy Halcyone. His beard and hair seemed wet and heavy with sea water. He leant over her bed, and his tears seemed to fall upon her face. "Do you recognize your Ceyx, my poor wife?" he said. "Or has death altered my face? Look at me and you will find not your husband, but his ghost. All your prayers, Halcyone, were of no help to me. I am dead. Do not hope any more. It is no use. The stormy wind caught my ship in the Aegean Sea and wrecked it. The waves filled my mouth, as I called uselessly your name. Now you must get up and weep for me. Put on a black dress and do not let me go unmourned to the shadowy world of the dead."

He spoke, and both his voice and the very gestures of the hands were exactly like those of Ceyx himself. Halcyone groaned in her sleep and stretched out her arms, trying to clasp them about his body; but it was only the empty air that she held. She cried out: "Stay! Stay! Where are you going? Let me go with you!" And then the sound of her own voice woke her up.

First she looked round to see if the vision was still there. Her servants had heard her voice and had brought in a lamp. When she could see no sign of him anywhere, she shrieked and tore her hair. Her nurse asked her what was the reason for her grief, and she said: "Halcyone has ceased to exist. She died when Ceyx died. Do not try to console me. He is shipwrecked and dead. I saw him just now and knew him and stretched out my hands to him as he went away, trying to keep him back. True, he had not got the bright look in his eyes which I know. He was pale and naked and his hair was all wet. He stood just here," (and she looked at the floor to see if he had left any footprints behind.) "This was just what I feared when I asked him not to leave me. Oh, how I wish that he had taken me with him! Then we should never have been separated in life, nor should we have been divided in death. Now my heart would be more cruel than the sea if it urged me to over-come my grief and to go on living. I shall not struggle with my grief, nor shall I leave you, my poor husband. Now at least I shall come and be your companion. If our ashes cannot rest in the same urn, our names will be written on the same tomb. If my bones cannot mingle with yours, at least the letters in which our names are inscribed will touch each other."

She could speak no more. Instead of words groans came from her despairing heart.

It was morning and she went out of her palace down to the shore, seeking again in her sorrow the place from which she had watched him sail away. While she lingered there and said to herself: "This was where he loosed his cable. This was where he gave me his parting kiss," and was bringing back to her mind everything that had happened, staring over the sea, she saw in the distance something which looked like a dead body, though at first she could not be sure what it was. The waves carried it nearer in, and, though it was still some distance away, it was clearly the body of a dead man. She did not know whose body it was, but, because it was a drowned man, she wept and cried out, "Ah, poor man, whoever you are! And poor wife, if you have a wife!"

The waves brought the body nearer and nearer. The more she looked at it, the more did she strain her eyes and the more did her heart beat. Now it was close to the shore: she could see it clearly. It was the body of her husband. "It is he," she cried, and, tearing her hair and her dress, she stretched out to him her trembling hands and said: "O Ceyx, dearest husband, is this the way that you come back to me?"

Near to the sea there was a breakwater that stood in the way of the first force of the waves. She ran to this breakwater and leaped out from it towards the sea. But she did not fall. As she leaped into the air she flew, and, with wings that had grown in an instant, skimmed over the surface of the waves in the shape of a bird. As she flew there came from her long pointed beak notes that seemed full of sorrow and complaint. But when she reached the silent bloodless body, she folded her new wings around the limbs that she had loved and, with her rough beak, tried to set kisses on his cold lips. It seemed to the people who were watching that Ceyx felt her touch, or perhaps it was the movement of the waves that had raised his head for a moment. But no, it was her touch that he had felt. Finally the gods had pity on them and they were both changed to birds. Their fates were inseparable; still, as birds, they are married; they mate together and bring up their young. And there are seven quiet days in the winter months when

Halcyone broods upon her nest that floats over the sea. At this season the waves of the sea are calm and still; for Aeolus guards the winds closely and forbids them to go out, making all the waters safe for his own grandchildren.

Oedipus

AFTER Apollo and Diana had entirely destroyed the race of Amphion, Thebes was without a king, and the people summoned Laius, a descendant of Cadmus, to come to the throne which, indeed, was his by right.

Laius had been warned by an oracle that, if he had a son, this son was fated to kill his own father. When, therefore, his wife Jocasta bore a son, Laius, in fear of the oracle, decided to put the child to death. Soon after the baby was born, a spike was thrust through his feet and he was given to a goatherd, who was told to leave the child on the cold steep slopes of Mount Cithaeron, where he would be devoured by wild beasts. The goatherd reported to the king that he had carried out his orders and the king's mind was set at rest. In fact, however, the man had not had the heart to destroy the small child and had given it to one of the servants of Polybus, King of Corinth, whom he had met on the mountain. This servant took the child to Corinth and there he was brought up and adopted by Polybus and his wife Merope, who were childless. They gave him the name of Oedipus, or "Swollen feet," because of the marks left on his feet by the spike with which they had been pierced.

So in Corinth Oedipus grew to manhood, believing himself to be the son of Polybus and Merope. He was distinguished in every way, and it was through jealousy of him that once at a feast a drunken young man mocked at him for not being the true son of his parents. Oedipus, in great anxiety, went to Merope and asked her for the truth. She attempted to set his mind at rest, but still he was not satisfied. He left Corinth alone and on foot, and went to ask the advice of Apollo's oracle at Delphi. What he heard terrified him. "Unhappy man," replied the oracle, "keep far away from your father! If you meet him, you will kill him. Then you will marry your mother, and have children who will be fated to crime and misfortune."

Now Oedipus believed that it was because of some knowledge of this dreadful fate that Polybus and Merope had given indefinite answers to his questions. He was determined not to do them any harm and vowed that never again would he set foot in what he believed to be his native city of Corinth.

So, still startled by the oracle's reply, he left Delphi, turning away from the sea and the way to Corinth, and traveling inland over the lower slopes of Mount Parnassus. On his left were the high mountains where eagles circled overhead; below him, on the right, was a long river valley where olive trees grew in such numbers that they themselves seemed a great flood of grey-green and silver flowing to the sea.

In the mountains there is a place where three roads meet, and here, as Oedipus was traveling on foot, he was overtaken by an old man in a chariot, with servants running at the side of the chariot. One of these servants struck Oedipus on the back with his staff, telling him rudely to make way for his betters. This was treatment that the young man, who had been brought up as a king's son, could not tolerate. He struck the servant down and killed him. He was then attacked by the old man in the chariot and by the other servants, and, defending his own life, he killed them all except for one who escaped and made his way back to Thebes with the news that King Laius had been killed. Since the man did not like to admit that he and the rest had been destroyed by one man singlehanded, he pretended that they had been attacked by a large band of robbers.

Oedipus, with no idea that he had killed his own father, went on his way in the direction of Thebes. He went past Helicon and came in sight of Mount Cithaeron, where, as an infant, he had been left to die. From the country people he learned not only that the King of Thebes had been killed, but that the whole land was terrorized by the Sphynx, a monster with lion's body and the head of a woman. The Sphynx guarded the approaches to the plain of Thebes. It had a riddle to which it demanded the answer from all whom it met. Already in the rocky plain were many piles of the bones of those who had failed to give the right answer, and now it had been proclaimed that if any man could answer the riddle and free the country of the Sphynx, he should have Queen Jocasta for his wife and himself become King of Thebes.

Oedipus resolved to make the attempt. Going out to a rock which towered above the plain, he found the Sphinx sitting on top of it, with great claws clutching the sandy ground. He demanded to know the riddle and the Sphinx said: "What is it that in the morning walks on four legs, in the midday walks on two, and in the evening on three?"

"It is Man," replied Oedipus. "In the morning of his childhood he crawls on hands and knees; in the midday of his youth he walks on his two legs; in the evening of his old age he needs a stick to support himself, and so goes on three legs."

The Sphinx, finding that at last her riddle was answered, threw herself down, as was fated, from the rock and died. Oedipus received his reward. He was made King of Thebes and took Jocasta, little knowing that she was his own mother, to be his wife. So the oracle was fulfilled, though none of those who had fulfilled it knew what the truth was.

Oedipus for many years ruled Thebes well and wisely. He was happy with Jocasta, who bore him four children—two twin sons Eteocles and Polynices, and two daughters Antigone and Ismene. It was not until these children had grown up that the truth was revealed and the happiness of Oedipus turned into the greatest misery.

Thebes, since the death of the Sphinx, had been prosperous and successful; but in the end a plague fell upon the land. The cattle died in the fields; blight fell upon the crops; then the people began to die, and the air was full of ravens and of vultures, ill-omened birds that came to feast upon the dead bodies of animals and of men. The people called in vain upon the gods to help. They looked

also to their king, who had saved them before from the persecution of the Sphynx.

Oedipus sent Creon, the brother of Jocasta, to the oracle at Delphi to ask the god how Thebes might be free of the plague. The reply came back that the plague had been sent because of the murder of Laius and because not even yet had the murderer made atonement for the bloodshed.

Oedipus immediately and with his usual energy began to make inquiries into the murder which he had himself unknowingly committed so long ago. He examined those who had heard the story at the time, and he sent for the old prophet Tiresias, whose wisdom was greater than that of mortals. The gods had taken away his sight, but had given him knowledge of the future and the past.

When the old man was summoned before the king, he had no wish to speak. "Let me go home again," he said, "and do not ask me these questions. It would be better, far better, for you to remain in ignorance. Take my advice, which is meant kindly to you."

But Oedipus, anxious for his people, and determined to show himself once more their deliverer, pressed on with his inquiries. As the old prophet still refused to speak, he began to grow angry, and to insult him. "Either," he said, "you are an old cheat who knows nothing, or else you have been bribed by the murderer to conceal his name, or else perhaps you are the murderer yourself. Either speak, or suffer every punishment that I can think out for you."

Then Tiresias spoke: "You yourself, Oedipus, are the man who murdered Laius. You murdered him in the place where three roads meet on the way from Delphi. It is because of you that the plague has fallen on this city. And there is worse news still that waits for you."

Oedipus remembered the old man in the chariot whom he had killed so long ago. He was horrified at the thought that he might have killed his wife's husband and began to question her as to his appearance and the number of his servants. As she answered him, he became convinced that the prophet had spoken the truth.

But Jocasta attempted to persuade him that Tiresias should not be believed. "Even Apollo's oracle," she said, "sometimes tells lies. For example Laius was told that he would be killed by his own son, but the only son we ever had was killed and eaten by the wild beasts on Mount Cithaeron."

Oedipus was interested by this story and demanded proof of it. The goatherd, now a very old man, who had taken the baby to Mount Cithaeron, was summoned. Oedipus questioned him closely and now, thinking that he had nothing to fear, the goatherd admitted that he had not killed the child, as he had been told to do. Instead he had given the poor weak thing to a servant of the King of Corinth.

As he spoke, and as Oedipus, in increasing excitement, went on questioning him, Jocasta suddenly realized the truth. Oedipus had been brought up by the King of Corinth, he still had on his feet the marks of the iron that had pierced them; it was indeed he who had killed Laius, and he who, fulfilling the oracle, had married his own mother. She cried out once. "I am an unhappy woman," she said, and then, looking for the last time on Oedipus, she went into the house. Then she tied her girdle to a beam, made a running knot in it, and hanged herself.

Meanwhile Oedipus was sifting the evidence of the goatherd. His keen intelligence saw how all the story fitted together, but only gradually could his mind grasp the truth —that, though he had never known it or suspected it, the words of the oracle had for long been proved, in fact, that he had killed his father and become the husband of his mother. As he became fully conscious of his own position, he heard a cry from indoors. There he found Jocasta dead, hanging from the palace roof. In misery, despair and shame, he took the pins from the buckle of her girdle and with them pierced his eyes. Then, with the blood streaming down his face, and with all the world dark to him, he came back to his people, resolved finally to leave them and to go abroad in exile, so that he might atone for the guilt which he had never imagined as being his.

His daughters, Antigone and Ismene, went with him, and for long, guiding the steps of their blind father, they wandered in the hills and valleys of Cithaeron and the mountains of Attica. In the end they came to Colonus, a little town near Theseus's kingdom of Athens. It is a town where fine horses are bred and where all the summer the tawny nightingale sings among the berries of the ivy that cloaks the trees. Here at last Oedipus found peace. Theseus gave him sanctuary, partly for his own sake, partly because an oracle had revealed that the land where Oedipus died would be famous and prosperous. Yet if Oedipus died at all, he died in a way that was miraculous. Theseus alone saw, or might have seen, the manner of his departing from life. For suddenly, in the sunshine and among the singing of the birds, the blind king began to feel the power of the gods upon him. He left his two daughters in the grove of Colonus and commanded Theseus to lead him forward over the rolling ground to the place where he had to be. Then, taking leave of Theseus also, he went on alone, with firm, though slow, steps, as though he still had the use of his eyes. From the clear sky came the roar of thunder and Theseus, in fear and reverence for the gods, hid his eyes. When he looked up again, Oedipus had gone, taken perhaps to Heaven or lost in some invisible fold in the ground.

In leafy, well-watered Colonus, and in Athens itself he received for ever the honors due to a hero, and to one whom, in the end, the gods loved.

The Seven Against Thebes

WHEN the blind Oedipus left Thebes the kingdom was divided between his two twin sons, Eteocles and Polynices. It was arranged that each brother should rule for a year, and, since Eteocles had been born first, he held the kingship for the first year. It was not long before it became clear that the hatred and jealousy which existed between the brothers would lead to trouble, if not disaster, for the city. Before the end of his first year of rule Eteocles drove Polynices from Thebes, intending to keep the royal power entirely in his hands.

Polynices, determined on his revenge, went to the court of Adrastus, King of Argos. Adrastus welcomed him, gave him his daughter in marriage and, with all his power, supported his claim to the throne of Thebes. First he sent to Eteocles the savage warrior Tydeus, an exile from Calydon who lived at the court of Argos, and was renowned both for his skill in battle and for his savagery. Tydeus, in the name of the King of Argos, demanded that Polynices should be restored to his country and to his royal rights;

Eteocles, however, replied that the wolf would make friends with the lamb sooner than he would forget his anger against his brother. He defied the King of Argos to do his worst, and sent out fifty men to ambush Tydeus on his return. Tydeus killed every one of them, and returned to Argos eager for war and for revenge.

Immediately King Adrastus planned an expedition against Thebes. There were seven captains of the army—Adrastus himself, his brothers Hippomedon and Parthenopaeus, his nephew Capaneus, Tydeus, Amphiaraus, and the claimant of the throne, Polynices. One of these seven, Amphiaraus, was not only a famous warrior but also a prophet. With his skill in prophecy he knew that of the seven captains in the Argive army, only one would return alive from the war. He therefore went into hiding, telling no one except his wife Eriphyle where his hiding-place was. Adrastus was now unwilling to make the expedition, since he had the greatest faith both in the generalship and in the wisdom of Amphiaraus. It was known that the prophet was entirely devoted to his wife. Polynices therefore determined to secure the help of Eriphyle.

At first she refused to tell where her husband was in hiding or to attempt to persuade him to join in a war which he knew would be fatal to nearly all the captains. But her vanity and her love for fine things proved stronger than her feelings for her husband. Polynices had brought with him from Thebes the famous necklace that Vulcan, the god of fire, had once made for Venus's daughter Harmonia, when she married Cadmus. Now he offered this necklace to Eriphyle as a bribe, and she, when she saw the flashing jewels and the varied lights that shone from each marvel-ously set stone, could resist no longer. She revealed where her husband was and herself joined King Adrastus and Polynices in persuading him to go to the war. Amphiaraus went, but he went unwillingly. He was angry, too, that his wife's vanity had been more powerful with her than her affection for himself, and he made his son Alcmaeon swear that, if he did not return, he would avenge his father's death by killing his mother.

So the great army, under its seven leaders, moved north-wards and camped on the slopes of Mount Cithaeron in view of the walls and the seven gates of Thebes. Eteocles with his army awaited the attack inside their walls. Before the coming battle he consulted the old prophet Tiresias and Tiresias said to him: "Great indeed is the army that is coming against you. There will be death upon death. As for Thebes herself, she can be saved only by the sacri-fice of the youngest child of Cadmus's blood."

Creon, brother of Jocasta and uncle of Eteocles, heard the words of the prophet with fear and horror. He knew that his own son, Menoeceus, was the youngest of the de-scendants of Cadmus, and he planned to have the boy sent out of the city into safety. But the young boy had him-self heard the prophecy of Tiresias. "I am too young to fight," he said, "but still I can be of more good to my coun-try than even the bravest fighting man." Then he ran to the wall and hurled himself down to his death among the army that was besieging his city.

Thebes itself was certainly saved. Each of the seven gen-erals of the Argive army led his force against one of the gates, but, after bitter fighting, each one was repulsed. Then Eteocles and the Thebans sallied out and fighting raged throughout the plain. Champions on both sides fell. The dusty ground was covered with the still or writhing bodies of men and horses. So great indeed was the slaughter that Eteocles sent a message to the invading army and proposed that the whole issue of the war should be decided by single combat between himself and Polynices.

Polynices welcomed the proposal, and the two brothers stood out alone between the armies for their last fight. So fiercely they fought that each seemed possessed by some god who fanned their unnatural anger into something more than human. The armies on each side stood applauding their own champions, but so even was the fight that none could say which of the two seemed likely to be the victor. At one moment it seemed that the force and fury of Polynices must be irresistible; at the next moment it appeared that Eteocles was on the point of beating down his enemy. Swords carved the flesh from arms and shoulders; blood streamed to the ground, and still the brothers fought grimly, neither giving way a foot. Even when loss of blood made their blows weaker, their anger was as strong as ever, and in the end each sank to the ground in death, each having won the victory and each having been defeated.

Instead of this double death being a signal for peace, it merely roused the two armies to greater ferocity. All day they fought and, as the prophet Amphiaraus had foretold, six out of the seven generals of the Argives lost their lives. Tydeus slew the Theban general who was opposing

him, but was himself mortally wounded. Before he died
he had brought to him his enemy's body which, in his rage,
he horribly maltreated. They say that the goddess Minerva
was on her way to help him and to make him immortal,
but that, seeing his cruel savagery, she turned away from
him and left him to his death. Amphiaraus himself died,
and before he died called upon the gods to witness the
treachery of his wife. His son, as he had promised, avenged
his father's death, and took back from his mother the fatal
necklace. Later he was pursued by furies, nor did the necklace bring him any good fortune.

Of all the leaders of the force of Argos, only King Adrastus returned. Thebes remained unconquered, but the victory had been bought at the price of the blood of its best
and strongest soldiers. Creon, uncle of the two sons of
Oedipus, became king. His aim was to restore the strength
of his city and bring back peace and good government
after the war; yet his first act was to bring more trouble
to the family of Oedipus and to himself.

Antigone

CREON became King of Thebes at a time when the city had lost half its army and at least half of its best warriors in civil war. The war was over. Eteocles, the king, was dead; dead also was his brother Polynices, who had come with the army of the Argives to fight for his own right to the kingdom.

Creon, as the new king, decided first of all to show his people how unforgivable it was to make war upon one's own country. To Eteocles, who had reigned in Thebes, he gave a splendid burial; but he ordered that, upon pain of death, no one was to prepare for funeral or even sprinkle earth upon the body of Polynices. It was to lie as it had fallen in the plain for birds and beasts to devour. To make certain that his orders should be carried out Creon set a patrol of men to watch the body night and day.

Antigone and Ismene, sisters of Polynices, heard the king's orders with alarm and shame. They had loved both their brothers, and hated the thought that one of them should lie unburied, unable to join the world of the ghosts, mutilated and torn by the teeth of dogs and jackals and by the beaks and talons of birds. Ismene, in spite of her feelings, did not dare oppose the king; but Antigone stole out of the city by night, and, after searching among the piled-up bodies of those who had died in the great battle, found the body of her brother. She lightly covered it with dust, and said for it the prayers that ought to be said for the dead.

Next day it was reported to Creon that someone (the guards did not know whom) had disobeyed the king's orders and scattered earth over the body of Polynices. Creon swore an oath that if the guilty person should be found, even though that person was a member of his own family, he or she should die for it. He threatened the guards also with death if they failed to find the criminal, and told them immediately to uncover the body and leave it to the birds and beasts of prey.

That day a hot wind blew from the south. Clouds of dust covered the plain, and Antigone again stole out of the city to complete her work of burying her brother. This time, however, the guards kept better watch. They seized her and brought her before King Creon.

Creon was moved by no other feelings than the feelings of one whose orders have been disobeyed. "Did you know," he asked Antigone, "the law that I made and the penalty that I laid down for those who broke the law?"

"I knew it," Antigone replied, "but there are other laws, made not by men but by the gods. There is a law of pity and of mercy. That law is to be obeyed first. After I have obeyed that, I will, if I may, obey the laws that are made by men."

"If you love your brother," said Creon, "more than the established laws of your country and your king, then you must bear the penalty of the laws, loving your brother in the world of the dead."

"You may kill me with your laws," Antigone replied, "but to me death is, in all these sufferings, less of an evil than would be treachery to my brother or cowardice when the time came to help him."

Her confident and calm words stirred Creon to even greater anger. Now her sister Ismene, who had at first been too frightened to help Antigone in her defiance of the law, came forward and asked to be allowed to share in Antigone's punishment; but Antigone would not permit her to claim a share with her in the deed or in its results. Nor would Creon listen to any appeal for mercy. Not wishing to have the blood of his niece upon his own hands, he gave orders that she should be put into an underground chamber, walled up from the light and then left to die.

So Antigone was carried away to a slow and lingering death, willing to suffer it, since she had obeyed the promptings of her heart. She had been about to marry Hacmon, the king's son, but, instead of the palace that she would have entered as a bride, she was now going to the house of death.

Haemon himself came to beg his father to be merciful. He spoke mildly, but let it clearly be understood that neither he nor the rest of the people of Thebes approved of so savage a sentence. It was true that Antigone had broken the law; but it was also true that she had acted as a sister ought to act when her brother was unburied. And, Haemon said, though most people did not dare oppose the king in his anger, nevertheless most people in their hearts felt as *he* did.

Haemon's love for Antigone and even his good will towards his father only increased the fury of the king. With harsh words he drove his son from him.

Next came the blind prophet Tiresias to warn King Creon that the gods were angry with him both for his merciless punishment of Antigone and for leaving the body of Polynices to be desecrated by the wild beasts and birds. Creon might have remembered how often in the past the words of Tiresias had been fulfilled, but now, in his obstinate rage, he merely insulted the prophet. "You have been bribed," he said, "either by Haemon or by some traitor to try and save the life of a criminal by dishonest threats that have nothing to do with the gods at all."

Tiresias turned his sightless eyes on the king. "This very day," he said, "before the sun sets, you will pay twice, yes, with two dead bodies, for the sin which you could easily have avoided. As for me, I shall keep far away from one who, in his own pride, rejects the gods and is sure to suffer."

Tiresias went away, and now Creon for the first time began to feel that it was possible that his punishments had been too hard. For the first time, but too late, he was willing to listen to the advice of his council, who begged him to be merciful, to release Antigone and to give burial to the body of Polynices.

With no very good grace Creon consented to do as he had been advised. He gave orders for the burial of Polynices and went himself to release Antigone from the prison in which she had been walled away from the light. Joyfully his son Haemon went ahead of the rest with pick-axes and bars for breaking down the wall. But when they broke the stones of the wall they found that Antigone had made a noose out of the veil which she was wearing and had hanged herself. Haemon could not bear to outlive her. He drew his sword and plunged it into his heart before the eyes of his father. Then he fell forward dead on the body of the girl whom he had wished to be his wife.

As for Creon he had scarcely time to lament for his son when news reached him of another disaster. His wife had heard of Haemon's death and she too had taken her own life. So the words of Tiresias were fulfilled.

Tereus, Procne and Philomela

TEREUS was a great warrior king of Thrace. Once he came from the north and helped King Pandion of Athens against his enemies. Though he was a barbarian, he was strong and wealthy, so that Pandion was glad of his alliance and allowed him to marry his daughter Procne. But neither Juno, the goddess of marriage, nor any god or goddess blessed this wedding. Nor did they bless the birth of the child Itys who was born to Tereus and Procne. Instead the screech owl sat upon their roofs and cried. This was the omen both for the wedding and for the birth. All Thrace, however, rejoiced at the alliance which Tereus had made, and, at the birth of Itys there were feasts held throughout the country.

Now four years passed and Procne said to her husband: "If you love me at all, either send me to visit my sister in Athens or else let her come to see me here. You can promise my father that after a short stay she will come back."

So Tereus launched his fleet and, with sail and oar, came to Piraeus, the port of Athens. As soon as he had met his father-in-law they clasped their right hands together and began their talk by wishing each other well. Tereus was telling how his wife desired to see her sister and would promise that she should return quickly, when Philomela, the sister of whom he spoke, entered the room. Her clothes were rich, but her own beauty was richer still. She was like a nymph of the woods or streams, except that she was better dressed and had more refined manners.

As soon as he saw her Tereus fell in love with her. In his wicked heart he desired her love rather than her sister's, and now he repeated Procne's message over and over again. As he spoke there were tears in his eyes, so that old Pandion and Philomela gave him credit not for his wickedness, but for a kind heart. Philomela herself, little knowing what was to come of it, put her arms round her father's neck, begging him for her sake as well as her sister's to allow her to go back to Thrace with Tereus. Her father gave her her own way, and the poor girl thanked him. What she thought would bring such pleasure to her and her sister would in fact bring ruin upon them both.

In the evening a royal feast was prepared. Wine was drunk from cups of gold. They rested, and next day Pandion took the hand of Tereus and, with tears in his eyes, said to him: "My son, it is natural for your wife to want to see her sister and for her sister to want to see her. Now I put Philomela in your care. Look after her well, and in a short time send her back to me to be the comfort of my declining years. However short a time she is away, to me the time will seem long."

Tereus made promises that he never intended to keep.

Now he felt wickedly secure of his prize, and as the ship cut its way through the blue sea to Thrace, he gazed at Philomela in the same way as a hungry eagle gazes upon a hare that he has caught in his hooked claws and dropped helpless into his high nest.

As soon as the boat reached the shores of Thrace, Tereus dragged Philomela off to a hut in the deep woods. There he shut her up, pale and trembling, frightened of everything and tearfully asking him where her sister was. And now he admitted his wicked purpose and forced her, alone and helpless, to be his wife against her will. When she reproached him for his treachery to her, to her father and to her sister, and threatened to tell everyone of his wickedness, both anger and fear drove him on to further cruelty. He bound her hands and with his sword cut out her tongue, so that she could never reveal to anyone what had happened to her.

Then, setting guards around the hut, he went to his palace where Procne was waiting for him, anxious to see both her sister and her husband. Tereus groaned aloud and told a false story of how Philomela had died on the journey. His pretended tears convinced his wife. She took her golden robe from her shoulders, and dressed herself in black. Also she built a monument to her sister's memory and made sacrifices to her spirit. True enough that her sister deserved to be mourned for, but not in this way.

A year went by. What could Philomela do? Guards and a stout wall of stone prevented her escape. Her speechless mouth could tell her tale to no one. Yet sorrow can sharpen the wits, and cleverness often comes to one's help in misfortune. On her loom she hung a Thracian web, and, weaving in purple on a white background, she told in pictures the story of how she had been wronged. Then, when the weaving was finished, she took the web from the loom and gave it to an old woman who was her own servant, begging her in gestures to take it to the queen. The old woman, not knowing what she was carrying, took it to Procne who unrolled the cloth, and read and understood the message that it contained. She did not utter a word, and it was strange that she was able to keep silent. Grief and anger made her speechless. Nor was there time for tears. She would mix right and wrong together, seeking revenge before anything else.

It was the time when the women of Thrace hold their feast to Bacchus on the mountains by night. There they dance and revel madly. No man at this time dares to stand in their way. And now Procne, dressed as a worshiper of Bacchus and surrounded by a crowd of women, rushed through the woods, pretending to be possessed by the god. She came to the hut where Philomela was imprisoned, swept aside the guards and then, hiding her sister's face and disguising her with wreaths of ivy, she took her back to her palace. Then she folded her in her arms, looking with pity on the sad and speechless figure that she had believed dead. They might for long have wept together, but Procne's anger was too great for this. "There is no room here for tears," she said. "A sword would be better, or something stronger than a sword. I am ready for anything —to burn the palace with my husband in it, or to cut him limb from limb, letting his wicked lifeblood flow away through a thousand wounds. I only hesitate to find what will give him most pain."

While she was speaking her son Itys came to her. Then she realized what to do and prepared a grim and terrible crime. Drawing a knife she killed the boy with one blow. Philomela cut his throat and together the two sisters cut the body to pieces. Then they roasted parts of it and boiled other parts in brass kettles on the fire.

This was the flesh which Procne invited her husband to eat. She pretended that it was a sacred feast at which only a husband was allowed to be present, and she made all the slaves and attendants go away. The savage king sat alone on his high throne. Then, when he had filled himself with the flesh of his own son, he said, "Bring Itys to me!"

Procne could not conceal her cruel joy. She longed to be the first to tell him the dreadful news. "If you want Itys," she said, "look for him inside your own body."

Then Philomela, with loose hair and hands stained with the blood, leaped forward. She could say nothing of what was in her heart, but she hurled the boy's head straight into his father's face.

Tereus sprang to his feet, overturning the table and crying aloud in his agony. Then he drew his sword and rushed at the two sisters.

They fled from him, and as they fled, they seemed to be flying on wings. And indeed they were. In the shape of birds one, Philomela, flew to the woods, the other, Procne, flew up to the roof. Now Philomela is a nightingale and still in song mourns for her cruel fate. Procne is a swallow

and bears still in the feathers of her breast the ma
blood. Tereus himself, as he sped in pursuit, was cha.
to a hoopoe. On his head there is a stiff crest, and inst
of his huge sword he has a long and curving beak.

Cupid and Psyche

PSYCHE was the youngest daughter of a king and queen. She had two elder sisters both of whom were remarkably beautiful. Their beauty, however, might be described in words. But the beauty of Psyche herself was past all description, as was the majesty of her bearing and her sweet and gracious disposition. So from all over the world people came to the country where she lived, merely to look at her. They looked at her with wonder and adoration, believing her to be either the goddess Venus herself, who was born from the foam of the sea, or else a new Venus, no less divine than the goddess of beauty and of love.

Thus the temples and ceremonies of Venus were neglected. People no longer offered sacrifices and prayed to her. Instead they thronged to visit Psyche, worshiping her as soon as she left her home in the morning, and laying garlands before her feet.

The true Venus was greatly angered by the neglect shown to her by men. "It is I," she said to herself, "to whom, on Mount Ida, Paris gave the prize of beauty. And am I to share my honors with a mere mortal girl? She will soon be sorry for being more beautiful than is allowed."

Then Venus called for her winged son, Cupid, the god of love, who with his arrows can conquer the gods themselves, who ranges over the earth like a bee, the brilliant and mischievous youth. "Now, my dear son," she said to him, "you must revenge the injury that is done to your mother. Mortals are worshiping this girl Psyche instead of me. I want you to make her fall in love with some wretched creature, poor and abject, the ugliest in the world. You with your bow and arrows can do this."

She took him then to the city where Psyche lived and pointed her out to him. Then she herself, after kissing her son, went to the shore near by, planted her rosy feet on the sea water, making it calm, and took her way over the sea to her sacred island of Cyprus. Around her played the dolphins and sea gods rose from the waves to make music for her on their horns of shell; nymphs of the sea came to shade her from the sun with their veils of silk or to hold before her eyes her golden mirror.

Meanwhile Psyche received no advantages from the adoration which was given everywhere to her extraordinary beauty. She was praised and worshiped, but no king or noble or even any common person came to woo her to be his wife. All wondered at her, but only as one might wonder at a picture or exquisite statue. Her two sisters, though less beautiful than she, had married kings. Psyche sat alone at home, hating the beauty which delighted everyone except herself.

In the end her father, suspecting that the gods must be envious of his youngest daughter, sent messengers to the oracle of Apollo to inquire what he should do. The reply of the oracle was: "Let Psyche be dressed in black, as for a funeral, and let her be placed on the top of the mountain that rises above your city. Her husband is no mortal being. He is like a dragon that flies in the night. The gods of heaven and earth, even the darkness of Styx, fear his powers."

Psyche's father and mother, who had been so proud of their daughter's beauty, now wept and lamented the sad fate that was in store for her. What the oracle commanded seemed more like death than a wedding. As they prepared to carry out the will of the oracle not only they, but all the people, wept continuously in mourning for the unhappy event. But Psyche said: "You should have wept before, in the time when everyone worshiped me and gave me the name of Venus on earth. Now you see what has come of my beauty. I am overtaken by the jealousy of the gods. Come now, lead me to the dreadful place. I myself long for this marriage I have been promised. At least it will end my unhappiness."

Then, in a great procession, most unlike a wedding procession, they took her to the wild rocky summit of the mountain. There were no glad songs or bright lights. Tears put out the torches. The people went back to their houses with bowed heads, and Psyche's wretched parents shut themselves for days in their palace, mourning for her fate.

Meanwhile Psyche was left alone, trembling and weeping, on the high rock. But there came a mild gentle breeze which softly lifted her from the ground and carried her, with her clothes lightly fluttering, gradually past the precipices and forests till it brought her to a deep and sheltered valley where she was laid down on a bed of grassy turf among the most beautiful and sweet-smelling flowers. This soft bed and the fragrance of the flowers calmed Psyche's restless and astonished mind. Soon she rose to her feet and saw in front of her a fine and pleasant wood with, in the middle of it, a running river as bright as crystal. And there among the trees stood a palace so beautiful that you would think it to be a mansion for one of the gods. The roof was made of citron and ivory. It was supported by pillars of gold. The pavements were of precious stones arranged by some great artist in the form of splendid pictures of animals, birds and flowers. The walls were built of great blocks of gold, and each door and porchway seemed to give out its own light.

The wonder of the place so enchanted Psyche that she boldly went inside and here again she found everything magnificent and looked lovingly at everything. There were fine storerooms full of rich dresses and of all kinds of wealth. What greatly surprised her was that in all the palace nothing was barred or bolted, nor was there anyone there to guard all these immense riches. While she stood still, half in amazement and half in delight at what she saw, she heard a voice, though no body was to be seen. "Why do you wonder, my lady, at all this wealth? It is all yours to command. We, whose voices you hear, are your servants and are ready to do everything you desire. Go therefore to your room and rest on your bed. Then tell us what kind of bath you wish to have prepared for you. Then, when you have refreshed your body, a royal dinner will be served."

Psyche, wondering still more, went to her room and rested. After a perfumed bath, she found the table all set for her convenience. Invisible hands brought her rare wines and delicious dishes of food. After dinner another unseen servant came and sang; yet another played on the harp. Then it seemed that she was in the middle of a great choir of voices singing most perfectly to the sound of all kinds of instruments. Yet singers and instruments were alike invisible.

As night approached, the concert of music ended and Psyche went to bed. Now she became frightened at the thought of the terrible husband promised her by the oracle; but again invisible voices assured her that her husband was one to be loved and not feared. When it was dark he came and lay down beside her. Though she never saw his face, she heard his voice and felt his body. In the morning he left before dawn, after telling her of his love and promising to return to her each night. So, though she was lonely in the day, she passed each day in great pleasure, being most pleased with the beautiful singing voices that surrounded her; and each night she spent with her husband whom she loved more and more.

Meanwhile her father and mother did nothing but weep and lament for their daughter whom they thought must certainly be lost for ever, either devoured by wild beasts

or by the terrible dragon. The news of her fate spread far
and wide, and Psyche's two sisters came to visit their parents and to mourn with them. That night Psyche's husband
spoke to her. He said: "My sweet love and dear wife, a
cruel fortune is bringing you into terrible danger, and I
wish you to be greatly careful. Your sisters, thinking that
you are dead, will come to the mountain in order to mourn
for you. If you hear their voices, do not answer them, for,
if you do, you will bring me great sorrow and bring yourself absolute ruin."

Psyche listened to him and promised that she would do
as he said; but, when he went away next day, she passed
all her time in weeping, and began to think that her fine
house was really no better than a prison, if she was allowed
to see no one and not even able to console her dear sisters
who were mourning for her. She ate nothing that day and
took no pleasure in her music. Red-eyed with crying, she
went to bed early. Her husband also returned earlier than
usual and at once he said to her, "Is this the way you keep
your promise, my sweet wife? Crying all day and not even
now comforted in your husband's arms? Do what you want
to do. You may remember my words too late, if you bring
on yourself your own ruin."

Then Psyche begged him more and more urgently to
give her what she wanted, that she might see her sisters
and speak with them. In the end he was won over by her
entreaties and told her that she should give her sisters all
the gold and jewels that she wished; but he earnestly en-
treated her never to be led by her sisters' advice into a
longing to see his own face. If she did so, he said, she

would lose the good life she had now, and would never feel his arms about her again.

Psyche was now full of gratitude and love for him. "I would die a hundred times," she said, "rather than be separated from you, my sweet husband. Whoever you are, I love you and keep you in my heart as though you were my own life. I could not love you more if you were the god Cupid himself. Now I beg you to let your servant the West Wind bring my sisters down to me here tomorrow, as he brought me." Then she kissed him and called him her sweet soul, her husband and her darling. He, such was the power of her love, agreed to do as she desired.

Next day her sisters came to the rock where Psyche had been seen last, and there they cried and lamented for her, so that the rocks rang with their cries. The sound came to Psyche's ears and she called back to them, "I whom you weep for am here, alive and happy." Then she called to the West Wind, who gently carried her two sisters down to the valley where she lived. For long there was nothing but embracing and tears of joy. Then Psyche showed her sisters her gorgeous house with its stores of treasure. She ordered the unseen musicians to sing; she feasted them with fine food and wine, and they (shameful creatures as they were) became filled with envy of her and determined in some way to ruin her happiness. Often they asked her about her husband, and Psyche, remembering the warning that she had had, pretended that she knew him by sight. He was a handsome young man, she said, with the down just growing on his chin, and his chief pleasure in the day was to go hunting in the mountains. Then, since she feared that she might make some mistake in her speech, she gave them all the gold and jewels that they could carry and ordered the West Wind to take them back to the mountain.

No sooner were they alone together than they each began bitterly and enviously to complain of Psyche's good fortune. "She is the youngest one of us three," said the older sister. "Why should she have a palace and stores of wealth? Why should she have those miraculous servants and be able to give orders to the West Wind? Indeed her husband may end by making her into a goddess. Even now she has every happiness. As for me, my husband is old enough to be my father. He is as bald as a coot and he keeps all his riches under lock and key."

The second sister was just as jealous as the first. "My husband," she said, "is always ill and I have to waste my time nursing him as though I were a doctor's assistant. I certainly cannot bear to see my younger sister so happy. Let us therefore tell no one of what we have seen; and let us try to think out some way in which we can do her harm."

So these unnatural sisters hid the gold and jewels which Psyche had given them. Instead of consoling their parents with the news of her safety and happiness, they pretended that they had searched the mountains for her in vain and that they were, with their sad faces, still mourning for her loss. Afterwards they went back to their own homes, and there began to think out plans by which they could somehow injure the sister whom they pretended to love.

Meanwhile Psyche's husband again spoke to her in the night. "My sweet wife," he said to her, "those wicked sisters of yours are threatening you with great evil. I think that they will come to see you again. Now I beg you either not to talk with them at all (which would be the best thing) or at least not to talk to them about me. If you obey me, we shall still be happy. Already you have in your body a child of yours and mine. If you conceal my secret, the child, when it is born, will be a god; if you do not, then it will be a mortal."

Psyche was very glad to know that she would have a divine child and was more pleased with her husband than ever. But her sisters hastened on with their wicked plots and, as they had arranged, came once more to the country where Psyche was. Once again her husband warned her: "Now is the last and final day," he said. "Now I beg you, sweet Psyche, to have pity on yourself, on me and on our unborn child. Do not even see these wicked women who do not deserve to be called your sisters."

But Psyche said, "Dear husband, you know that you can trust me. Did I not keep silent before? Let me at least see my sisters, since I cannot see you. Not that I blame you for this, and indeed darkness is like day to me when I hold you, who are my light, within my arms."

With such words she persuaded him once more to order the West Wind to carry her sisters to her. Before dawn he left her, and early in the day her sisters were brought to the soft and fragrant valley and to her palace. They were gladly welcomed as before by Psyche, who told them proudly that before many months she would become a mother. This made the sisters more jealous than ever, but they hid their feelings beneath smiling faces and began to ask her once more about her husband. Psyche, forgetting that before she had told them that he was a young man, now said that he was a great merchant from a nearby province, and that among his brown hair he had a few hairs of grey. Instantly the two sisters, when Psyche had left them for a moment alone, began to say that she must be lying. "Perhaps," said one of them, "she has never seen her husband. If so, then he must be one of the gods and she will have a child who will be more than mortal. How can we bear this, that our youngest sister should have everything? Let us at once think out some lies by which we may destroy her."

So they spoke together, and when Psyche returned to them she found that they were both weeping. Not knowing that their tears were all pretended, she asked them in surprise what had happened. "Poor Psyche," they said, "you who do not know the face of your husband, it is terrible for us to tell you the truth, but we must do so to save your life and the life of the child who will be born to you. The real shape of your husband is not what you think at all. No, it is a great and savage snake that comes to you every night. Remember the oracle that said you would be married to a fierce dragon. The country people have often seen him, swimming through the rivers as he returns at evening. They say that he will wait a little longer and then eat both you and your child. We have done our sad duty in telling you of this. If you are wise, you will take our loving advice and escape from your danger while you still may."

Poor Psyche in her simplicity, believed in the false story

and in her sisters' love. "It is true," she said, "that I have never seen my husband's face, and he tells me that something dreadful will happen to me if I try to see it. Oh, what am I to do?"

Then her sisters began to work still more upon her fears. "We will help you in this, as in everything," they said. "What you must do is to take a knife as sharp as a razor and hide it under your pillow. You must have hidden also in your bedroom a lamp with oil ready for burning. When he comes to bed and his limbs are all relaxed in sleep, you must get up quietly, on your bare feet, light the lamp, and, holding the knife firmly, cut off the head of that poisonous serpent just where it joins the neck. If you do this, we will come back to you next day. We will take all the riches out of this house and marry you to some real man who is not a monster."

Then these wicked women left her, and Psyche, trembling and shrinking from the thought of it, still prepared to do what her sisters had advised. Night came, and her husband, after he had kissed her and taken her in his arms, soon fell asleep. Psyche, made bold by her fear, yet still scarcely able to believe that what her sisters had told her was true, slipped from the bed, grasped the knife firmly in her right hand and took the lamp, hardly daring to wonder what she would see when the lamp was lit. What she saw was no monster, but the sweetest of all things, Cupid himself, at whose sight even the lamp burned more brightly. His hair was gold and seemed itself to shine; his neck was whiter than milk; the tender down on the feathers of his wings trembled with the light movement of his breathing and of the air. For long Psyche gazed in love and wonder at the beauty of his divine face, his smooth and soft body. In shame at what she had thought of doing she turned the knife against herself, but the knife shrunk from such a dreadful act and slipped from her hands. At the foot of the bed were Cupid's bow and arrows, small weapons for so great a god. Psyche took them up and, as she tried the sharpness of an arrow on her finger, she pricked herself. Then of her own accord she fell in love with Love and she bent over the bed, kissing him in joy and thankfulness as he slept.

As she was doing so a drop of burning oil fell on the white shoulder of the sleeping god. He woke and saw that she had broken her promise and her faith. Without uttering a word he fled away from her kisses and her embraces; but she clung to him, following him out of the great palace and crying to him.

Then he alighted on the top of a cypress tree and spoke angrily to her: "O foolish Psyche, think how I disobeyed the orders of my mother, who told me that you should be married to some base and worthless man, and instead of this I came myself to be your husband. Did I seem a monster to you that you should try to cut off my head with its eyes that love you so much? Did I not warn you often of this? Your sisters will suffer for what they have done. You too will suffer from not having me with you."

He flew away through the air and Psyche, as long as she could see him, kept her eyes fixed on him as he went, weeping and crying for him. When he had gone beyond her sight, in her despair she threw herself into the running river; but the gentle stream would not take her life; instead it set her on the bank, where again she lamented what she had lost.

The sun rose in the sky and Psyche, weary and wretched, turned away from the palace where she had lived, and wandered through forests and rocky ways aimlessly, except that her aim was to find somehow, if it might be possible, her husband again. In her wandering she came to the city where the husband of her eldest sister was king. She could not forgive her sister's treachery, and now she pretended to be more simple than she really was. To her sister's questions she replied, "I took your advice, my dear sister, but, when I raised the lamp, I saw no monster but Cupid himself. Because of my disobedience he has left me, and he said that instead of me he would have you as his wife."

No sooner had Psyche spoken these words than her sister, without offering Psyche herself any help in her distress, hurried away from her home and came to the mountain as she had done before. There was no West Wind blowing, but in spite of this the greedy and deceitful creature threw herself down, crying out: "Now Cupid, I come to you. Take me to yourself as a more worthy wife." Instead of the gentle passage through the air which she had expected, her body was torn and broken on the rocks. Wild beasts and birds tore it limb from limb and devoured it. The other sister suffered the same fate, for Psyche, in her wanderings came also to her city and told her the same story that she had told to the elder of the two. Her greed and folly were the same, and she had the punishment that she deserved.

So Psyche went through country after country looking for her husband Cupid. He, however, was resting in his mother's house, ill and suffering from the wound in the shoulder which had been made by the burning oil. Nor did his mother Venus yet know anything of what had happened. But a talkative white gull came to her as she was bathing on the seashore and told her of how Cupid was wounded and how he had lived in marriage with her enemy Psyche. At this news the anger of Venus grew greater than ever it had been. "Will he," she said, "not only disobey his own mother, but actually fall in love with this wicked girl whose beauty was said to be equal to mine? I shall lock him in the house and make him suffer for it. As for the girl, I shall find her and make her wish she had never set eyes upon my son."

Then she mounted her glorious chariot of gold, thick set with precious stones. Four white doves drew the chariot lightly through the air; sparrows chirped merrily around it, and there followed flocks of all kinds of singing birds, who, being in the choir of Venus, had no fear of hawks, eagles or other fierce birds of prey. So, as the clouds yielded before her, Venus went on her way to heaven and there she complained to all the gods and goddesses of her son Cupid and of his love for Psyche. The others, and especially Juno and Ceres, tried to soothe her anger, partly because they were afraid of Cupid themselves; but Venus refused to be comforted, and ordered her servants to search for Psyche throughout the world.

Meanwhile Psyche, tired out with her wandering and with the weight of her child that had not yet been born, visited the temples of all the gods, asking them for their help. Juno and Ceres indeed would have wished to help her, but they did not dare to offend Venus. Though all pitied her, none would give her rest and sanctuary, so that in the end Psyche decided, in her despair, that she would go to the house of Venus herself. "Perhaps," she thought, "my mother-in-law will forgive me and have pity on me. Perhaps I shall see my husband. Then at least I shall die happy. And in any case my life is now unbearable."

Venus, when she saw the girl for whom she had been so long searching, laughed cruelly at her. "So you have at last decided to come and call on me, have you?" she said. "I suppose you are thinking that, just because you are going to have a baby, I shall be glad to be called a grandmother! You wicked immoral girl, I shall soon show you what I think of you."

Then she leaped on Psyche, tearing her clothes and pulling her hair and knocking her head upon the ground. Afterwards, with her fierce cruel anger satisfied, she put in front of her a great pile of wheat, barley, millet, poppy-seed, pease, lentils and beans. She said, "You are so ugly that no one could want you for your face. Possibly you might find a husband by being a good housewife. Let me see what you can do. I order you to separate all these different grains, each from each, before I come back from dinner." Then Venus, putting garlands on her bright gold hair, went away to a great banquet and Psyche sat in front of the heap of grain, weeping to herself since she knew that her task was impossible.

But a little ant took pity on her. He went out and spoke

to all the other ants saying, "My friends, let us help this poor girl who is the wife of Cupid and in great danger of her life." So the ants came and with their quick careful labor soon neatly separated the grains each in its own pile.

At midnight Venus returned, all fragrant with perfumes and well warmed with wine. When she saw how the work was done, she said: "This is not your doing, you vile wicked thing. It must be the work of him who loves you." Then she threw Psyche a crust of brown bread and she saw that Cupid was locked in the most secure room of the house. So these two, who loved each other, spent separate and sad hours in the same house.

In the morning Venus came to Psyche and said, "You see that river over there, with reeds and bushes along the banks. By the river is a flock of sheep which have fleeces gleaming with gold. Go and bring me back some of their wool."

Psyche rose from the hard floor and went out. Her real wish now was to throw herself in the river and die; but when she reached the river a tall green reed, by divine inspiration, spoke to her and said: "Poor innocent Psyche, do not stain my holy water by your death. But do not go near those terrible wild sheep until after the middle of the day. Till noon they are fierce and will kill anyone who comes near them. Afterwards they will rest in the shade and you may easily go up to them and take the wool which you will find hanging on the briars."

Warned by this gentle reed, Psyche did as she was advised and in the afternoon came back to Venus with her apron full of the wool from the golden fleeces. Venus still frowned at her in anger. "This again," she said, "is no work of your own. Now I will prove whether you have the courage that you pretend to have. Do you see that overhanging rock at the top of the great mountain over there? From that rock gushes out a stream of black and freezing water that feeds the rivers of Hell, Styx and Cocytus. Go to the very summit and bring me a bottle of water from the middle of the source of the stream."

Psyche climbed the mountain, but when she drew near the summit she thought indeed that it would be better to hurl herself down on the rocks than to proceed any further with her task. The black stream ran in great foaming cataracts, or slid over slippery stone. Even the force of water and the rugged steep slopes were enough to make her journey impossible. Then on each side of the stream she saw great dragons creeping over the hollow rocks and stretching out their long necks. Their sleepless eyes never ceased to watch the sacred water, and the water itself foamed and bubbled with voices all saying, "Go away! Go away! Fly or you will die."

Psyche therefore stood still, weeping at the hopelessness of what lay before her. But Jupiter's royal eagle saw her and wished to do good to the wife of Cupid. He flew past her face and said to her, "Poor simple girl, do you think that you can even approach these terrible waters that are feared even by the gods? Give me your bottle." Then, taking her bottle in his beak, he flew past the darting tongues and flashing teeth of the dragons, plunged the bottle in the stream and brought it back filled with the water of Styx. Psyche took it back to Venus, who again looked angrily at her and spoke harshly. "You must be," she said, "some sort of a witch or enchantress to carry out my orders so quickly. Well, there is one more thing that I want you to do. Take this box and go down to Hell, to the dwellings of the dead. There you are to ask Proserpine, the Queen of Hell, to send me a little of her beauty, just enough to last for a day. Tell her that I have lost some of mine in looking after my son who is wounded. But you must return quickly, as I have to go to the theater of the gods."

Now poor Psyche felt that all pretense was over and that she was surely doomed to die. She knew of no way of going to the House of the Dead except by killing herself, and so she climbed a high tower, resolved to throw herself down from the top. But the tower spoke to her and said: "Do not yield, Psyche, to this last and final danger. If you kill yourself, you will indeed visit the world of the dead, but you will never come back to this world. Listen to my words and do as I say. Not far from here is Taenarum where you will find a great hole in the ground. Go down the path bravely and it will lead you to the very palace of Pluto. But you must not go empty-handed. In your hands you must carry two cakes of barley and honey mixed. In your mouth you must have two halfpennies. When you have gone some way on your journey you will see a lame donkey carrying wood and a lame man driving him. The man will ask you to help him pick up some of the sticks that have fallen, but you must go on without a word, and do no such thing. Then you will come to the river of the dead where the foul old man Charon with his leaking boat ferries the souls between the banks. He will do nothing unless he is paid, and you must let him take from your mouth one of your two halfpennies. When you are on the black and deathly river you will see an old man swimming there who will beg and pray you to help him into the boat. You must not listen to him, since this is not allowed. When you have crossed the river you will pass by some old women weaving. They will ask you to help them, but you must not listen to them. These are all traps which Venus will set for you so as to make you drop one of the cakes from your hands. Yet without these cakes you can never make the journey or return again; for you will come to the great three-headed watchdog Cerberus, whose barking rings for ever through this desolate plain. He will never let you pass till you have given him one of your cakes to eat. Once you have passed him you will come into the presence of Proserpine and she will offer you a fine chair on which to sit and fine food to eat. But you must sit upon the ground and ask only for brown bread. Then tell her why you have come and receive what she gives you. On your return give the other cake to Cerberus and your other halfpenny to grim Charon. Then you can come back to the upper air by the same way as you went down. Above all, do not look inside the box that Proserpine will give you. There is no need for you to have any curiosity about the treasure of heavenly beauty."

So the tower advised Psyche, and she took the two halfpennies and the two cakes and then made her way to Taenarum. She descended the dreadful path to Hell, passed by the lame donkey in silence, paid her halfpenny to Charon, gave no attention either to the man swimming in the river or to the women weaving, gave one of her cakes to the terrible watchdog and came finally into the presence of Proserpine. Here she refused the fine food that was set before her and sat humbly on the ground, asking only for a crust of bread. Then she gave Venus's message and received the secret gift in the closed box. On her way back she gave the cake to Cerberus and her last halfpenny to Charon. So she reached the upper air in safety, but then she said to herself, "What a fool I am to be carrying in this box the divine beauty and not to take a little of it for myself. If I take some I may please my husband in the end."

She opened the box but could see no beauty in it at all. Instead a deadly sleep came over her like a cloud and she fell fainting to the ground, lying where she fell like a dead body.

But Cupid was now cured of his wound, and, in longing for his wife, had climbed out of an upper window. He flew straight to her and, when he had wiped away the deadly sleep from her face and put it back in the box, he woke her by gently pricking her hand with one of his arrows. "Poor creature," he said, "again you were nearly ruined by your excess of curiosity. Now go back to my mother and leave me to arrange the rest." Then he flew into the air and Psyche brought the box to Venus.

Cupid meanwhile flew up to heaven and begged Jupiter, the father of the gods, to help him in his faithful love. Jupiter called all the gods and goddesses to council and said to them, "It is not good that Cupid should be always loose and wandering about the earth. He has chosen a wife and it is right that he should enjoy her company and her love.

In order that the marriage shall not be an unequal one I shall make Psyche immortal, and she and Cupid will live together in happiness for ever. This is my will and, since Psyche will be a real goddess, even Venus must be glad of the marriage."

Then he sent Mercury to bring Psyche up to heaven and, when she had come there, he said, "Take this cup of immortality, Psyche, and drink it to the end, so that you may live for ever and that Cupid may never leave you again, but be your everlasting husband."

Then the great feast and wedding banquet was prepared. Cupid and Psyche sat in the places of honor and by them were Jupiter and Juno and all the gods in order. Bacchus filled their glasses with nectar, the wine of the gods. Vulcan prepared the supper. The Hours and Graces adorned the house with roses and other sweet-smelling flowers. Apollo and the Muses sung together and Venus danced with divine grace to the music. So Psyche was married to Cupid and in time she bore a child whom we call Pleasure.

TABLE OF NAMES

Many of the characters in this book were known by two different names, one of them Greek and the other Latin. Below is a list of the main examples.

LATIN	GREEK
Aurora	Eos
Bacchus	Dionysus
Ceres	Demeter
Cupid	Eros
Diana	Artemis
Jove *or* Jupiter	Zeus
Hercules	Heracles
Juno	Hera
Mars	Ares
Mercury	Hermes
Minerva	Athene *or* Pallas
Neptune	Poseidon
Pluto	Hades
Pollux	Polydeuces
Proserpine	Persephone
Ulysses	Odysseus
Venus	Aphrodite
Vulcan	Hephaestus

REX WARNER (1905–1986) was a novelist, translator of Latin and Greek, and scholar of classical literature. A member of the Auden generation, Warner wrote several darkly allegorical novels, most notably *The Aerodome*, before turning to historical fiction and in 1960 winning the James Tait Black Memorial Prize for his *Imperial Caesar*. Warner was a translator of Xenophon, Thucydides, Plutarch, Caesar, and St. Augustine as well as the poet and Nobel laureate George Seferis, whom he befriended while acting as Director of the British Institute in Athens in the years immediately following World War II. After teaching literature at Bowdoin and the University of Connecticut, Warner returned to England in the 1970s.

EDWARD GOREY (1925–2000) was born in Chicago. He studied briefly at the Art Institute of Chicago, spent three years in the army testing poison gas, and attended Harvard College, where he majored in French literature and roomed with the poet Frank O'Hara. In 1953 Gorey published *The Unstrung Harp*, the first of his many extraordinary illustrated books, which include *The Curious Sofa*, *The Haunted Tea Cosy*, and *The Epiplectic Bicycle*.

*Other New York Review Books Classics**

*For a complete list of titles, visit www.nyrb.com or write to:
Catalog Requests, NYRB, 1755 Broadway, New York, NY 10009-3780

fortune. On her loom she hung a Thracian web, and, weaving in purple on a white background, she told in pictures the story of how she had been wronged. Then, when the weaving was finished, she took the web from the loom and gave it to an old woman who was her own servant, begging her in gestures to take it to the queen. The old woman, not knowing what she was carrying, took it to Procne who unrolled the cloth, and read and understood the message that it contained. She did not utter a word, and it was strange that she was able to keep silent. Grief and anger made her speechless. Nor was there time for tears. She would mix right and wrong together, seeking revenge before anything else.

It was the time when the women of Thrace hold their feast to Bacchus on the mountains by night. There they dance and revel madly. No man at this time dares to stand in their way. And now Procne, dressed as a worshiper of Bacchus and surrounded by a crowd of women, rushed through the woods, pretending to be possessed by the god. She came to the hut where Philomela was imprisoned, swept aside the guards and then, hiding her sister's face and disguising her with wreaths of ivy, she took her back to her palace. Then she folded her in her arms, looking with pity on the sad and speechless figure that she had believed dead. They might for long have wept together, but Procne's anger was too great for this. "There is no room here for tears," she said. "A sword would be better, or something stronger than a sword. I am ready for anything —to burn the palace with my husband in it, or to cut him limb from limb, letting his wicked lifeblood flow away through a thousand wounds. I only hesitate to find what will give him most pain."

While she was speaking her son Itys came to her. Then she realized what to do and prepared a grim and terrible crime. Drawing a knife she killed the boy with one blow. Philomela cut his throat and together the two sisters cut the body to pieces. Then they roasted parts of it and boiled other parts in brass kettles on the fire.

This was the flesh which Procne invited her husband to eat. She pretended that it was a sacred feast at which only a husband was allowed to be present, and she made all the slaves and attendants go away. The savage king sat alone on his high throne. Then, when he had filled himself with the flesh of his own son, he said, "Bring Itys to me!"

Procne could not conceal her cruel joy. She longed to be the first to tell him the dreadful news. "If you want Itys," she said, "look for him inside your own body."

Then Philomela, with loose hair and hands stained with the blood, leaped forward. She could say nothing of what was in her heart, but she hurled the boy's head straight into his father's face.

Tereus sprang to his feet, overturning the table and crying aloud in his agony. Then he drew his sword and rushed at the two sisters.

They fled from him, and as they fled, they seemed to be flying on wings. And indeed they were. In the shape of birds one, Philomela, flew to the woods, the other, Procne, flew up to the roof. Now Philomela is a nightingale and still in song mourns for her cruel fate. Procne is a swallow